FAMILY KNO-

"What's going

"I've been on t   lied.
"There was an ad in *Scene*. a   metal
group needs a girl to front for them. They're a
guitar short, too."

Joe tried to remain calm. There goes Patti again,
wanting total control. "What group is that?"

"The Hunz-z. H-U-N-Z-Z."

"What about Benji?" Joe asked stonily.

"Already packed."

"You ain't taking Benji. He ain't going on the
road again. Not with some metal band."

"He's my son, remember?" she shouted. . . .

ROUGH DECISIONS

☐ **THE BEST THAT MONEY CAN BUY by Anne Snyder and Louis Pelletier.** Angie is used to having everything—lots of money, a luxurious home, an exclusive private school, a gorgeous boyfriend—until her father is accused of fraud and her charmed life suddenly begins to crumble.... (135938—$2.50)

☐ **NOBODY'S BROTHER by Anne Snyder and Louis Pelletier.** 16-year-old Josh suffers from a severe stuttering problem—with everyone except his 11-year-old stepbrother Howie. But now their parents are getting a divorce, and Josh faces the toughest dilemma of his life: he must choose between two people he loves very much. (117565—$2.25)

☐ **YOU WANT TO BE WHAT? by Anne Snyder and Louis Pelletier.** Joey has been a professional model since he was ten years old, but now he is rich, sexy, and seventeen—and his sights are set on beautiful Donna and a career as a stuntman. Except that he can't imagine what the people who call the shots for him will say.... (132203—$2.25)

☐ **ALICE WITH GOLDEN HAIR by Eleanor Hull.** Slightly retarded, Alice has been living in an institution since her mother's death years before. Now she is eighteen and the people at the home think she can handle a job—but will she be able to learn so many new things and face the responsibilities? Terrified, Alice soon discovers that sometimes being special is more important than being smart. (117956—$2.25)

Prices slightly higher in Canada

LIGHT
OF DAY

A Novel by
Robert Feiden

Based on the Motion picture written by
Paul Schrader

A Taft Motion Pictures/
Keith Barish Productions Presentation

A SIGNET BOOK

NEW AMERICAN LIBRARY

PUBLISHER'S NOTE

This book is a work of fiction. Names, characters, places, and incidents either are the product of the author's imagination or are used fictitiously, and any resemblance to actual persons, living or dead, events, or locales is entirely coincidental.

NAL BOOKS ARE AVAILABLE AT QUANTITY DISCOUNTS WHEN USED TO PROMOTE PRODUCTS OR SERVICES. FOR INFORMATION PLEASE WRITE TO PREMIUM MARKETING DIVISION, NEW AMERICAN LIBRARY, 1633 BROADWAY, NEW YORK, NEW YORK 10019.

SIGNET TRADEMARK REG. U.S. PAT. OFF. AND FOREIGN COUNTRIES REGISTERED TRADEMARK—MARCA REGISTRADA HECHO EN CHICAGO, U.S.A.

SIGNET, SIGNET CLASSIC, MENTOR, ONYX, PLUME, MERIDIAN and NAL BOOKS are published by New American Library, 1633 Broadway, New York, New York 10019

First Printing, February, 1987

1 2 3 4 5 6 7 8 9

PRINTED IN THE UNITED STATES OF AMERICA

LIGHT
OF DAY

1   "We gotta get out of here" Patti Rasnick said as she sat alone in her 1975 Nova.

"Here" was Cleveland, and for a long time the dismal dull color of steel gray had clouded the city. It was a place of factories and foundries, smokestacks and tank farms, a supplier of rubber and steel, whose black engines of industry exhaled white streams of smoke into the fluorescent sky. But in 1987, there was the hope of something more, and the chance of breaking away. Hope and promise played on the radio. All you had to do was turn it on and the volume up, all the way up.

"Rock and Roll!!!"

Kid Leo and all the other disc jockeys knew it.

They spread the hope. They played the music. And they promised that Cleveland was the home of the music the Midwest needed.

Sure, the competition was fierce. Not any band could make it beyond the walls of the countless clubs and bars. You had to believe you could make it, and you had to want it more than anything else. New names and new bands were there to remind you that it could happen: R.E.M., the Cure, the Cult, the Bangles, Motley Crue, the Dream Academy, and always Springsteen, Cougar, Benatar, and Seger. Rock and Roll! That could make the difference. Waiters, checkout clerks, parking lot attendants, and kids in school all knew it. And their hope found its way onto one of that summer's most popular T-shirts, emblazoned with the words, BUT MOST OF ALL, I WANT TO PLAY GUITAR.

Across the country, in every city, there were thousands of kids in hundreds of bands who dreamed of making it big in rock and roll. But the goal of getting a nationwide three-minute hit record is a slow, arduous process that can take years—if it happens at all. Usually bands have to develop a local or regional following first.

Cleveland had become a city that was just as good, if not a better, place to begin.

The Barbusters were from Cleveland.

Patti and Joe Rasnick, sister and brother, were the leaders. Patti was tough and wiry, the kind of girl who can't remember a time when she wasn't called sexy. Her mane of jet-black hair, teased and spiked for concerts, always seemed either to attract the wrong guys or to intimidate the right ones. Joe always thought his sister was cool, even though she could suddenly betray herself by letting her anger surface. Yet that's what Joe envied most—her energy. Once she strapped on her guitar, stepped into the light, and started to sing, no one could say the raven-haired rocker wasn't the best thing to hit Cleveland in years.

Joe's looks were in sharp contrast to Patti's, but he had the same drive on stage and off. He was a short, slight twenty-two-year-old with long brown hair and an open, friendly face. Like his sister, he was passionate about music and life, but he knew there were times when Patti snapped and needed to depend on someone else's strength. Joe was always there for her, though he wasn't sure she knew how strong he truly was. Ever since Patti was in her teens, Joe could remember her saying, "I can take care of myself." And sometimes she could. But not always.

The Barbusters were rounded out by three of Joe and Patti's best friends: Bu Montgomery was a tall, easy going guy who played bass, Billy Tettore, the spiky-haired youngest member at eighteen, kept the pounding beat on drums. And Gene Bodine was the sound engineer and roadie, but he had such energy and enthusiasm that the group considered him a full-time member.

Like all bands, the Barbusters knew the rules of playing rock and roll. You don't need a college education. There are no exams to pass. You can be rich or poor, of any race, religion, or even sexual preference. Nothing is quite so democratic. All you have to be is terrific. Being good isn't enough. And your chances are better if you're good-looking, play with superior skill and passion, and write hit songs. You must also be willing to do things you don't really want to in order to survive. And sometimes bands have to do things they know are wrong.

For Joe and Bu, the time between gigs and practice was spent at Marsh Allan Products, Inc., a sprawling, impersonal metal factory. The routine was endless and grinding.

Joe's radio alarm jolted him awake with a blast of guitars and drums at 6:00 A.M. The first thing he saw were rock posters covering all four walls and the ceiling of his bedroom. These glittering images were in sharp contrast to the tedious workday ahead—row after row of older men, their pasts behind them and no future ahead, toiling over metal presses and bulky crates. There were guys the same age as Joe and Bu, but most of them either had no further ambition or had resigned themselves to following the drudgery of their older relatives, often working side by side with them at the plant. At least Joe and Bu had the hope of something better: making it as a band. That dream sustained them.

4

Before leaving the house each morning, Joe looked in on Patti's son Benji and kissed the sleeping boy good-bye. After chugging a cup of coffee, Joe drove across town to pick up Bu. He often imagined Bu and his wife Cindy sitting down together for a hot breakfast. That was a distinct advantage to having an old lady, Joe thought: breakfast.

Work at the plant was tedious, but everyone had to pay their dues. Workers even formed an unofficial fan club. None of them truly believed anything would come of Joe and Bu's "hobby," but they could be relied on to show up at gigs here and there, pay the admission charge, drink endless pitchers of beer, and rowdily cheer their friends on.

Much of the applause, of course, was meant for Patti. At twenty-five, Patti was already a star in the eyes of many local men. The fact that she was unmarried and had a four-year-old son only added to her mystique.

Gene Bodine worked at a card and novelty shop in Randall Park Mall. The twenty-year-old blond hunk usually showed up in cutoffs and tight scruffy T-shirts, but the customers didn't seem to mind. Certainly not the women, whom Gene always called "chicks," regardless of age. The chicks often asked his advice on which cards to buy, and he enjoyed flirting with the young ones who would ask him if he thought their boyfriends would prefer this or that card. Once in a while he scored with them, the solitary bonus for a lousy wage.

Billy Tettore sat in his high school classroom carving a swastika on his desktop. It wasn't that he was a neo-Nazi (or even, for that matter, knew what one was); it was simply one of many punk mannerisms he picked up and then discarded just as quickly.

Patti spent her days keeping house and looking after Benji. There was always MTV or a soap opera to watch while cleaning, although Benji already preferred MTV so he could play along on his toy guitar. To break the monotony, Patti took Benji on an afternoon excursion that was a routine in itself. They would shop, return cans and bottles at the Pick-n-Save, and then stop at the magazine store to flip through her favorites, oblivious to the THIS IS NOT A LIBRARY; NO BROWSING sign. If she had enough packages in her arms, it was easy for Patti to rip off a fan magazine or two. What was she to do? She couldn't stand there and read all day, and she did have to keep up on her reading and research into current hits, looks, and trends.

Joe was standing at his place behind a "stamping" machine, one of his least favorite duties.

Cafeteria-style trays were fed from a long conveyor belt to a slot right in front of him. As each tray passed by, Joe lowered the stamper, making an imprint on the metal platter. The designs were always tacky and slightly midwestern, so Joe was used to them, but even he had to laugh at the latest one—a blurry picture of Prince Charles and Lady Di smiling brightly, their wedding date emblazoned beneath. Who buys these things, Joe wondered, fighting the impulse to look up at the enormous wall clock. Somehow the time went faster if he didn't allow himself to keep checking the minutes and the hours. But he couldn't resist any longer. It was four-thirty—only another half hour! His eyes locked with Bu's, and they exchanged big grins and thumbs-up signs. It was almost the end of the day, the end of another week, and tomorrow Joe and Bu, Billy and Patti would be together rehearsing. Being with the Barbusters was the only time they all felt really alive.

There's something eerie about a half-empty club while a band rehearses. The Euclid Tavern was no exception, though it was definitely a bar, not a club. People didn't go to hear rock and roll; they went to hear rock and roll while they drank.

Factory workers and a few unemployed youngbloods sat at the bar, some smoking cigarettes in silence, others mumbling to one another. But for

Patti, arching her back and clutching the mike, it didn't matter. She just loved to sing, and in her sweat-stained white T-shirt and jeans, she imagined she was singing to a packed house. She closed her eyes and suddenly she was in front of a sold-out crowd at CBGB's in New York. She had never been there, of course, but she had heard of it and seen pictures in rock magazines. But as the song ended, so did her dream. There was no reaction from the customers.

"Hey, Oogie," Patti sarcastically called to the bartender, "thank your friends for the support." Oogie just shrugged.

Joe and Bu began disconnecting their guitars. "Hey, what's wrong?" Patti asked. Billy started playing drums again, and Patti sang to his lone accompaniment.

"I promised I'd meet Cindy at the mall. I'm late already," Bu called as he packed his guitar.

"That's what I love about rock and roll—commitment." Billy smirked, not missing a beat.

"Go home and play in front of a mirror." Bu laughed. "I've already rehearsed past my deadline."

Patti stopped singing and walked over to Bu. He was right. She put her hand on his shoulder and smiled a silent thanks.

"Oog? Who you got coming in tonight?" Patti called.

"Yogurt Moon."

"Yogurt Moon?" Patti and Joe gave each other a look.

"Yeah, they used to be the Clones," said Gene as he picked up guitar cases. "They're from Shaker Heights. Daddy bought 'em uniforms so they went psychedelic." He made a disdainful face when he mentioned the wealthy suburb. Shaker Heights was synonymous with well-trimmed lawns, well-dressed people, and an easy life. One of the two girls shooting pool stopped and put a quarter in the jukebox. The screech of heavy metal chased the stillness from the bar.

"I know them," said Joe, "They worked for free at Cheers."

"Fuck," yelled Bu. "No wonder we could only get a hundred! Are we paid up front this weekend? Visa won't let me slide anymore."

"Damn straight," volunteered Patti. "Right Oog? Because we know the magic words!"

"Rock and roll!" they screamed.

"Party!" They put their arms around each other.

"Cleveland!" And they burst out laughing.

"Never fails," Patti said to Oogie, giving him a wink.

2 Joe and Patti lived in a small white tract house in Cleveland Heights. The dingy little room was constantly cluttered with sheet music, magazines, toys, and instruments. Curtains hung limply on sagging rods, and murky sunlight filtered through in spots on the floor. The carpet was frayed and stained—but clean, Patti always insisted. The lamps were old hand-me-downs from family and friends and none of them matched. A couple of posters and a Barbusters flyer were all that covered the paint-chipped walls.

Today, Joe practiced his guitar on the dilapidated couch, wearing nothing but a pair of faded gym shorts. He was alternately reading *Penthouse* and watching MTV with his feet propped up on a footlocker coffee table, while Benji banged on his toy guitar.

"Be careful, Bongo Boy," Joe cautioned Benji. "You'll break it."

Patti entered from the kitchen, wiping her hands on her jeans. She walked over to Benji and caressed his head. Joe looked up and smiled. He loved the little boy so much he felt more like a father than an uncle.

"Is that the Tears for Fears video?" asked Patti.

"Looks like it."

"What happened?" She smirked good-naturedly. "Bored with 'The Love Connection'?" MTV video jock Mark Goodman appeared on the screen droning on about Whitney Houston. "Ugh. When they goona get rid of him?" Patti sighed as she noticed Joe reading *Penthouse*. "You agreed not to read that around Benji!"

"What?"

"P-E-N-T," Patti sang.

"I'm not looking at the pictures. Honest."

"That's beside the point. It still makes an impression." Joe tucked the magazine under a cushion as Benji smacked a chord and started singing, "P-E-N—"

"Cut that out." Joe laughed. Benji, defiant, threw his guitar to the floor. Patti picked it up and gently handed it back to him. "Be nice to me, will ya, Patti? I got anxiety. I don't know if I can relate to fourteen-year-olds anymore."

Patti picked Benji up and signaled Joe with her eyes. He turned off the television and looked at the boy. "Benji, the TV's off. You know what that means, don't you? It means it's bedtime." Benji frowned in protest. "Don't give your mother a hard time. I know for a fact that she has something special to read to you. And if you're good, she may even sing something."

As Patti turned to take Benji upstairs, she asked Joe if he was going out. "You kidding? I barely dragged my ass through today. I'm shit-faced tired."

"Well, I may."

There was an awkward pause as Joe glanced at his sister, knowing the topic he was about to bring up was a touchy one. "Patti, we gotta get a present for mother's birthday," he started hesitantly. "Any suggestions?"

Patti shot Joe a stare.

"Sorry I asked," Joe muttered.

Patti grabbed Benji up in her arms and turned abruptly on her heels. At the foot of the stairs, she softened for a minute and told Benji to blow a kiss to Uncle Joe. The boy puffed up his cheeks and blew; Joe slapped his cheek and fell to the floor as if the kiss had knocked him over. Benji giggled, then he and Patti disappeared up the stairs.

Joe returned to the sofa and fished his copy of *Penthouse* out from under the cushion, opened it, and gave the centerfold an appraising glance. He read for a few more minutes, then dozed off. When he awoke, he slipped groggily upstairs and tiptoed into Benji's room. Benji was rolling about, snuggled up to his stuffed animals in bed. What a kid, Joe thought. He gave Benji a kiss on the forehead, stumbled into his own bedroom, and flopped down on the bed. He was too tired to undress.

As he lay there, Joe remembered Patti's cold stare at the mention of their mother's birthday. Mother's birthday, Joe thought. An occasion. And that usually meant trouble. Visits back home to Mom and Dad were never easy. But Joe craved sleep now. He didn't want to lie awake in bed thinking and worrying about it. But he did just that.

Joe thought about Patti and the troubled relationship she had with their mother. Throughout her childhood, Patti had been no more difficult than most kids. Her conflicts and arguments with her parents were nothing out of the ordinary. Neither Patti nor Joe shared their parents deep religious beliefs. But their parents became concerned when Patti and Joe started talking about rock and roll as more than a hobby. Patti had taken to rock music before Joe, and their parents cited this as an example of Patti's bad influence. The Rasnicks thought that music was a waste of time, and certainly nothing they had ever hoped for their children as a real career.

The worst arguments started after Patti had become pregnant. She refused to identify the father and insisted she was going to have the child and raise it by herself. Joan Rasnick couldn't imagine what she or her husband had done wrong in raising Patti. How could a daughter of theirs have let such a thing happen? How could Patti be so naive as to think she had a meaningful life ahead of her? What would she do and where would she go? It was one thing that neither Patti or Joe had gone to college. That had been a terrible disappointment for their parents. But Patti pregnant? This was an affront Joan Rasnick just couldn't abide. And why wouldn't Patti discuss it, or even tell them who the father was? Joan could not help Patti if she insisted on being so stubborn and obstinate. And why was Patti so angry with Joan? What had *she* done?

When Patti made it clear that she didn't want her mother's help, and when the quarrels became more and more intense, Patti moved out. Shortly thereafter, Joe moved out also, taking a room in Patti's house. Another example of Patti's bad influence! Joe had to get a job right away at a factory. What kind of future was that? Joan Rasnick was certain that Patti's recklessness had destroyed both her children's lives. But after Patti gave birth to Benji, Joan found that she couldn't just abandon them. She and Ben, her husband, would be there. Maybe it wasn't really too late after all.

Maybe her children would come to their senses and try to make something of themselves. And now there was a grandchild for Joan to think about. That child would need Joan and Benjamin's help, too. If Patti had emerged an unfit daughter, who was to say what kind of mother she would be?

Joan searched for the meaning of God's will in all of this. Nothing that she could think of led her to expect that this was what she deserved. Her children had been raised in a house overflowing with lessons and teachings of God's expectations for His followers. Joan would have to wait and see, and continue to pray.

More often than he liked, Joe found himself in the role of mediator between Patti and their mother. He loved his parents, but he also loved his sister. He had always looked up to Patti, and somehow, being her younger brother and part of the same generation as his sister, Joe didn't condemn her actions. He was more understanding and accepting. And, maybe most of all, there was the common bond of music. Rock and roll was part of Patti and Joe's times, and it had become the passion of their lives. That was something their parents might never understand.

Joe finally fell asleep.

Patti sat at her bedroom bureau applying makeup. She was glad that Joe had decided to stay home. More than any other time, Patti liked the night, especially the early morning hours. Joe would be sleeping by now. The house was deathly silent. Patti grabbed her black leather jacket and put it on as she walked back downstairs and out of the house.

The Rascal House video arcade was filled with the buzzing sounds and flashing lights of video games; even the blast of heavy metal muzak couldn't compete. She could hear the mix of noises as she got out of her car and walked past the local teenagers standing next to their parked motorcycles.

Inside, the air was thick with teen sex, as school kids stood squeezed in front of machines with names like "Scorcher," "Gorgar," and "Vulgus." Patti walked straight to an "Infraspace" machine and slammed a tall stack of quarters on the control panel. She made no attempt to see who was there, or even to make eye contact with anyone. The blank look on her face as she manipulated the joystick didn't invite anyone to approach her. Ping! Pong! Ping! Patti seemed to absorb the sounds. For now, at least, she didn't have to think about her mother's birthday. Or about anything at all. This was better than being angry.

For now, Patti was where she wanted to be: in the zero zone.

3 "One minute," Patti called to Joe as they were getting ready to leave. "I almost forgot Ma's birthday present."

"That's sweet," Joe said, dreading this visit to their parent's home, but impatient to get it over with. "I can just see us getting there, and at the big moment, guess what? Surprise: Patti forgot the present."

"Don't be so self-righteous. You never even thought to ask what I picked out. It's a housecoat. Pink."

"Listen, Patti, it's just that I'm on edge. You know what these family functions are like. You and Mom at each other every other second."

"I don't like it any more than you do. I can't

19

help it. You know they don't give a damn about our band. I think they're embarrassed by what we do. It's not like they're ever gonna ask us to play some new demos for them."

"You expect too much at this point, Patti. They're not going to change about that. Let's just try to have a nice day."

The truth was that Joan Rasnick cared very much for her two children. And on this day, her fiftieth birthday, she found herself filled with concern that the house and dinner be just right for them. It might as well have been *their* birthdays. For Joan, it was enough that today was a day that the whole family would be together, no matter what the reason. She must be sure to wake her husband from his nap so that he'd be ready when they arrived. Benjamin was so easygoing, so content. His chief pride was that he was head of a household. Unlike Joan, Ben never seemed to worry; he took each day as it came. He never looked back or further ahead than that evening's television schedule. He was a factory worker with a family, and that was that. He left for work each morning knowing Joan would be there at the end of the day with dinner prepared. He drew strength from that sense of regularity and permanence; he drew strength from the house itself; but mostly he drew his strength from Joan. As long as Joan was there, everything else would fall into place.

Joan and Benjamin had known each other since

their teens. Their families had been dirt farmers in the hills of Kentucky. At school Benjamin was just about as withdrawn as he was now. Nothing seemed to interest him—farming least of all, to the disappointment of his own father. He did his schoolwork and often returned right home, preferring not to take part in after-school activities. He was often too shy to attend class dances. His classmates found it odd that he kept so much to himself, but after many attempts they gave up inviting him to join them for after-school sodas or nights at the movies. Inside, Benjamin wanted success, but he could never fathom just what he wanted to do to achieve it. This career uncertainty also upset Benjamin's parents. They were fundamentalists, and even though their son willingly went to services with them, they sensed his restlessness at church. They asked their minister to speak to him, to try to break through. Sometimes they took Benjamin's isolation as a sign that perhaps some religious vocation awaited him. But Benjamin equivocated.

Nothing caught his interest until he looked up from his desk one day at school and a new girl walked into class. This was Joan, and from the moment he saw her, Benjamin Rasnick had something—someone—to think and care about. But it was Joan who had to introduce herself first. She was indeed a beautiful girl. There was a freshness and a spirit to her, and the kids at school couldn't imagine what she saw in Benjamin. But she pursued him. The only painful thing for Benjamin was that Joan had accepted her parents' fundamentalism in every way. She believed in God and destiny, and she was sure she and Benjamin belonged together. She felt almost a duty to draw him out of himself. And even though he revealed little of himself at first, Joan could sense what she called a "goodness" about him.

She spoke of a purpose in life, of a greater plan God had for every human being. As a result of her deep interest, Benjamin realized how much he really didn't like being alone. He knew he felt different when he was with her, and he knew this peppy woman was the one he would marry. Joan too felt some area of the ministry would be right for Benjamin and she coaxed him in that direction. He would think about it. He would read the literature she gave him. But first he was determined that they would marry, and then they would move away from farm country. He had heard that Cleveland was a place where a young man could make a steady living. Others he had known had moved there. All practical considerations were thrown aside and Benjamin and Joan were married within the year. Soon after, they moved to Cleveland. A couple of years later Joan gave birth to Patti, their first. Economic necessity forced Benjamin to continue as a factory worker, a job he had first taken "just for a while." But he never thought about what else he could do. He was content just providing a home and seeing his wife and Patti. And then, several years later, Joe was born. Life seemed complete.

Joan Rasnick was the spirit and backbone of her family, and that light glowed in her face. It was a face imbued with a special grace and gift; it was filled with empathy. She listened attentively and with concern. Sometimes Benjamin was amazed at her patience with other people's problems, often as seemingly insignificant as the moan of despair from a fellow cardplayer dealt a bad hand. Her manner was easygoing and ebullient, and she always seemed to be looking for a cause, for people to help. She participated in church functions and charity bazaars. Benjamin couldn't understand how she could respond with such inordinate glee to winning a recipe contest. And although she allowed Benjamin to mold areas of her exterior life, she seemed to have maintained her deepest and innermost beliefs.

Her interior life was filled with religious conviction. She firmly believed God and His will, took solace in her religious readings—and not just the Bible. She subscribed to numerous religious journals, often underlining pertinent points so that if the need arose she could look them up. Sometimes, when Benjamin was troubled, she would go to her special bookshelf and read to him, trying not to notice that his gaze became distant and tired when she did so.

*   *   *

Joe's blue Chevy pulled into the drive of the modest house in Lakewood, a well-kept middle-class community in West Cleveland. Each home was a success story; each represented the land of promise. Now, Joe, Patti and Bongo Boy walked into the house. Joe, carrying the present, was dressed in jeans and a sportcoat. Benji was in an Oshkosh outfit, and Patti had on her ubiquitous motorcycle jacket. The front door was open and they let themselves into their parents' living room.

Joan flew from her chair and embraced her children. "Oh, how good you're here! I've been counting the minutes. I'm sure I made your father very nervous, what with my asking him the time over and over again. And look at my grandson! Handsomer every day. Gosh, I wish we were all together more often, don't you, Ben?" Ben offered an understated welcome and did not bother to get up from his favorite Queen Anne chair. Patti, Joe, and Benji went to sit in their predetermined spots on the sofa alongside the Magnavox.

Joan went into the kitchen and returned with a tray of coffee and little cakes. "The ones with the frosting are for Benji." She laughed. Patti and Joe shot each other a look as if to acknowledge their father's silence. They were used to this by now. More often than not, he said and showed nothing.

"How were the roads?" Joan asked.

Patti, puzzled, looked out the window at the

clear summer weather. "Terrible," she answered sarcastically. "Downpour. Hail as big as a baby's fist. Euclid Avenue was under a foot of water."

Joan glared at Patti; the tension was palpable. Patti and her mother regarded each other with suspicion, opponents in an unspoken battle. It was left to Joe to break the tension.

"It was fine, Mom. No problems." Joe looked to his father. Ben Sr. motioned Benji over; his grandson joined him. This man needed a hug.

"Last time everyone was here it was raining," Joan said, not wanting to seem a fool who spoke out of no experience of these matters.

"And how are you, Dad?" Patti asked.

"Can't complain." Although Patti had hoped to open a conversation with her father, she realized this was the best he would do for now. But an undercurrent of feelings between Patti and her father *did* exist, feelings never spoken, never to be spoken.

Joan took the opportunity of silence to break in. "You know how I love you children. It's so rare to have everybody in the house at the same time— even though we live so close. I thought last year at Christmas—"

Joe nodded and sipped his coffee. In moments like these, he couldn't tell if his mother was dotty or simply inane. "We were working," he interrupted.

"I don't understand why anyone would want to

work on Christmas. I mean that is the most wonderful day of the year." She bit her lip and thought for a moment. "It's such a treat to have everyone together. Your father and I really appreciate it. We really miss seeing you."

Religious periodicals lay neatly across the coffee table. Joe paged through one, until he realized he wasn't at all interested. "Maybe this year," he said, putting the magazine back in its place.

"You don't know how happy it makes us to be all together."

Patti turned to Joe and whispered, "She says that one more time and I'm gonna dance to it". Patti stood up and looked at a framed relief map of Ohio.

Once again, Joan explained, "Yes, but it's so nice having *everybody* here." Patti turned to Joe. An awkward pause—then Patti, as promised, started to dance—bop. Then she sang, "Bop, bop, shoo-bop."

Joe turned from her, supressing a grin. "Yes, it is, Ma. It really is."

"Maybe it's time to move to the dining room. I for one am hungry. And if we don't go now, Patti's likely to dance herself to death."

The Rasnick dining room looked as if it might have been decorated by a minister who had suddenly learned that his true calling was interior design. Sixties bric-a-brac cluttered the room, laminated plaques, a calendar and slogan stickers, and an assortment of family photographs. Sentiment, not style, was important here.

The family sat around the remains of a birthday cake. The family was laughing at one of mother's anecdotes. She was a natural storyteller; just enough truth, just enough exaggeration. The punch line always seemed irrelevant.

". . . it's true, honest. Dogs can tell if a person's lying. I mean its master, of course. Not just anybody. You couldn't just take a dog up to anybody on the street and see if they are lying. Otherwise the police would be doing that. It's got to do with your voice—the vibrations or something." There was a comic pause for objections.

Joe teasing, asked, "Did someone tell you this at the beauty parlor?"

"No, as a matter of fact. Who can believe what you hear at a beauty parlor!"

"Then it must have been 'Merv Griffin'."

Even Patti joined in the banter. "I know, a 700 Club!"

"No, I *read* it."

"In the *Star*," Joe chided.

Patti couldn't resist. "I know. I remember it now. It was 'Donahue.' I saw it myself. With the sound off. A woman with a Pekingese."

Joan smiled slyly and winked at Bongo Boy. "Nobody takes me seriously around here, did you notice that?"

"It *was* 'Donahue,' " he chirped.

Everyone laughed as Joan rolled her eyes heavenward. "Don't *you* start on me . . ." Then she stopped and thought for a moment, suddenly exclaiming, "He's right! It was 'Donahue'!"

The laughter died down as Joan cast a mildly disapproving glance at her daughter, who was already attacking her full plate with a knife and fork. "Patti?" she said sweetly. "We forgot to say grace."

The group resumed their seats and lowered their heads. Joe folded Benji's hands. Father looked from Mother to Patti. He knew what was coming. Mother began, "Our Father who are in heaven, we thank Thee for bringing us together safely. We thank Thee for watching over our house . . ." Patti and Joe exchanged glances. Patti tensed. "We ask Thee to watch over Patti, Joe, and little Benjamin. Grant them health. Help them through their trials and tribulations. We particularly ask Thy help for Patti. We ask Thee to show her a special measure of grace . . ."

Patti was about to explode. Joe tried his best to calm her, mouthing the words, "Take it easy. Cool it." Patti clenched her hands, hoped against hope she could endure.

"Help her understand. Guide her ways. Forgive the sins of her youth, the mistakes . . ."

That did it! Patti slammed her knife down, stood up, and bolted out of the room. All Joe and Benji could do was watch. Father glanced up, winced, and lowered his head again. Mother, oblivious, continued. "We know Thou are all-forgiving." Joe released Benji and followed Patti out of the house. Joe grabbed his sister just as she went to open the car door.

Patti spoke with almost demonic fury. "I told her. I warned her. I was real clear. I told her if she mentioned church or rock and roll or marriage, I'd walk out of the room if I was in it, hang up the phone if I was on it. She just can't bring up those subjects no more."

"Calm down, Patti. It was just prayer."

"That's her trick. Thought she could get away with it. No way. It's her or me. There's no middle ground."

"Patti, have some compassion. It's her *birthday*."

"That's why I agreed to come. I knew she'd try to pull something like this."

"Patti, she's getting old."

"You give her an inch . . ."

Trying to break her anger with a joke, Joe said, "And she takes a yard. Just like crabgrass." There was no reaction from Patti. "Patti, that was a joke, a bad one maybe, but a joke. Lighten up."

Patti cooled down somewhat. "She's trying to destroy us, Joey. Music is all that matters. One hour on stage makes up for the other twenty-three." And Patti felt the reality of this more than ever. She couldn't live for her mother's blessing or approval. If that made her a rebel, so be it. But

29

the birthday experience had one benefit: Patti was firmer now in her conviction. Her brother could come along or stay out. There was no existing in both worlds.

Joan and Benji appeared at the front door. Benji, crying, clutched his grandmother's leg. Father watched from the living room, in profile. Her mother's forlorn stare only agitated Patti more. Joe eased Patti into the driver's seat. "I better go back. I'll tell her something."

"I'm sure you will. You'll take Benji back?"

Joe nodded as Patti started the engine and floored the accelerator. Her fury subsided as she drove. She could sense it turning into something else—something more real, more vital, more meaningful. What she felt now was an ambition. The odd thing was that the feeling that filled her was both frightening and calming all at once. With a quick glance in the rearview mirror, she saw her family fade until they were no longer there. She drove onward. She was headed into the future, and a part of her—a real part—sensed that her dream was waiting just around the corner.

4 The light of day was beginning to fade into a humid Cleveland night. Joe sat behind the wheel of the parked Nova. All his energy seemed to be equally divided between the concentrated anxiety in his forehead and his fingers, which were impatiently beating out a rhythm on the steering wheel.

He glanced to his right where Bu sat slouched against the door. What were they doing here? How had he let Patti talk him into this?

Across the street a couple stood on their porch with the harsh light glaring down on their faces, and a halo of bugs dancing behind them. They appeared to be arguing, their voices low and their movements stiff. Finally the husband turned away and began walking down the steps. He raised his voice as he moved toward their car.

"Don't start with the blue suit again."

Her heels clicked across the pavement as she scuttled after him. "Don't talk to me like that! I was only saying it would be nicer if we matched . . ."

Bu shifted in his seat and rubbed his eyes. "This is really dumb."

"I never knew you had a problem with dumb," Patti shot back.

"That's normal dumb. This is really dumb."

Joe glanced at Patti, then turned away with a smile. Here it was a sweltering night and Patti had her old leather motorcycle jacket on. Leave it to Patti to sacrifice comfort for appearance.

Outside the husband was whining, "What do you mean? Why do we always have to be color-coordinated?"

"Listen, Patti said it'll only take five minutes," Joe whispered. "The cellar door is always open. We just pick up their tools, and Patti swaps them for the Peavy sixteen-channel amplifier we need." He sounded almost confident, the way he always felt when he invariably took his sister's side.

"Do it," Bu said evenly. "Alone."

"Somebody has to stand watch," Joe pleaded. "Just honk twice."

"Hey Bu. Cut the crap. You said you wanted to come," Patti chided.

"Yeah, but I thought we were going for burgers or something. Not rip off a house. I love ya, Patti, but I'm gone. Tomorrow. Gotta put in some time at home anyway." Bu got out of the car, and was just as quickly out of sight.

"Patti, he's got a point."

"This was your idea too. You've been talking about this Peavy amplifier for weeks."

"Can't I change my mind?"

"We gotta get out of here." Patti's mood had become tense.

"I know."

"Outta this town, I mean. Outta Cleveland. We've got to get a better sound. You know we need new equipment."

"Okay, okay," Joe agreed.

But just then, the marital quarrel erupted again. "Let's just go and have fun!" the husband barked.

"How do you expect me to have fun when you're constantly pulling away from me?" She was near tears as she whirled around and ran back up to the house. Her husband threw his hands up in disgust, then lowered his head and followed her inside. The light went on.

"Damn!" Patti cursed.

"Sis, I'm splitting. They're back inside and they're not leaving. Are you coming?"

"Wait a little longer."

"Nope, I'm splitting. Now." And with that Joe purposely hit the horn twice.

"Very funny," Patti called out after him as she heard his footsteps echo down the blacktop. Patti kept her eyes on the house. She suddenly knew that the tool heist was out of the question, but she didn't budge. It was a point of honor. Sometimes she felt so much more determined than Joe. Or was it just rebellious? Rebellious. How many times had she heard her parents call her that? But all she could ever remember wanting to do was to sing rock and roll. She could feel the frustration making her whole body hot as she stared stonily ahead and muttered, "We gotta get out of here!"

5   It was Monday again, time for the Barbusters to begin their various daytime rituals. Days were endured without passion, but they led to the freedom of night and rehearsals. And maybe some gigs.

At 7:00 A.M. ("the crack of ice," Patti called it), Joe pulled the Chevy in front of Bu's brick apartment house. Lunch box in hand, Bu walked drowsily to the Chevy and got in. Entering the Marsh Allan Products plant sparked no energy, only the conversational drone of sleepy men as they shuffled past the hand-lettered sign over the doorway: PERFORMANCE IS A REFLECTION OF ATTITUDE. Joe took his place next to Bu at the retread sorting line, pulling a pair of headphones from his pocket.

Bam! The factory noises were totally replaced by the aggressive chant of Ian Hunter's 1978 rock anthem, "Cleveland Rocks." Joe's face was transformed by the blast of music. This was always his first big smile of the day.

In the stockroom of the card store, Gene opened his lunch bag. He saw two yuppie wives discussing scented candles. He unwrapped his sandwich and punched the boom box beside him. Bam! "Cleveland Rocks."

Billy, in a health and safety class, tried to listen to the lecture on sexual responsibility. As the teacher turned his back to write on the board, Billy jammed his transistor earplugs into his ears. Bam! "Cleveland Rocks."

Patti was spending the afternoon at home with Benji. Restless, she alternately read fan magazines and watched television. Actually, she managed to do both at once. She had turned to the local news program, which was showing a news story about unemployment and other depressing economy-related subjects. Patti cursed to herself and jumped up to turn the dial to MTV. A band played while one surrealistic set replaced another in the background. Nothing depressing about this, Patti thought, lighting a cigarette. And suddenly she felt a mood change. Depression had now led to envy. "We gotta make it, we gotta get *there*," Patti said aloud, pointing her cigarette at the television screen.

Saturday afternoon was equipment repair day at Joe and Patti's house. The Barbusters looked forward to these times. They would eat lunch in the backyard—grilled franks and burgers or Kentucky fried chicken. But it was the talk they enjoyed the most: conversation about their hopes and dreams and how they were going to make it. The talk often turned to opinions and good-natured arguments about new bands, new hit records. Like most bands who had yet to make it big, the Barbusters found it easy to fault other's successes. New acts were dismissed as being yesterday's news or "toy," a word that had come to mean the most forgettable of a band's music. Patti, in particular, found most new bands toy.

Gene, Billy, and Bu sat on the back lawn uncoiling and rewinding cable. Benji, wearing an IT'S O.K. I'M WITH THE BAND T-shirt, tried to catch the attention of a cocker spaniel that drifted in and out of the yard, oblivious to the child's antics. Next door, neighborhood kids were playing on swings.

Inside the garage, Patti and Joe labored over stacks of equipment: four Marshall speakers, a BGW 750-power amp, a Crown 150. The garage served as a workshop/storeroom for the band; used and defunct equipment filled the room. A bag of rusting gold clubs rested atop broken toys and appliances. Patti held a light as Joe soddered a crossover connection on the amp rack.

As he worked, Joe was telling Patti about something that happened the other day. "Just go down to Randall Park Mall. Look at all the people, all dressed in different clothes, all thinking different things—yet all trying to be happy. Just think about it. All over the world, billions of people, every one of them, trying to be happy. And she said, 'Wow! I didn't know rock and roll players were so deep!' " Patti and Joe broke up laughing.

"This is Sue Pisarick's friend?" asked Patti. "What is she, sixteen?"

"She's older than that. She's seventeen."

"Sue's seventeen. This girl's a year younger."

"But have you seen this girl? So beautiful . . ."

"So dumb!"

"Bright like a night-light . . ."

"No cheekbones. In ten years, Edsel face!"

Joe continued working. "I swear God must be perverse. He just sits around dreaming up these beautiful woman, sends them down here to make us feel like shit, then gives 'em zip for brains so they run off with the first dealer they meet. It's the angels. They drive Him buggy."

"She'll break your heart," Patti teased.

"Please," Joe said playfully as he clutched his chest.

"Get Sue to set you up."

"You kidding? You born yesterday?"

"Yeah," Patti said in her best catty voice. "I'm Patti: day two."

"She hates me. I'm serious."

"I'm Patti." She extended her hand and they laughed. "Okay, look, I'll set you up. I know her sister. Besides, she doesn't hate you." Patti ruffled Joe's hair. "Nobody hates you." Just then a soldered connection broke.

"Sonofabitch," cursed Joe.

"If we had taken those tools and got the Peavy, we wouldn't need this."

"Nonsubject," said Joe, trying to dismiss the thought of the abandoned burglary attempt.

"What's with the halo number?" Patti shot back. "You've done you're share of 'creative borrowing.' "

"It's just you gotta be more careful. At first it's fun, then each time it's something more."

"Do I have to hear this?" Patti was angry now. "What's next? The part about little brother's paycheck and how you support the band?"

"I thought we were talking about Sue Pisarick's friend?"

"Twelve-track music. One-track mind."

Joe looked up, relieved to see someone coming. "Here comes Cindy." Cindy Montgomery, twenty-eight, Bu's wife, in her nurse's uniform, walked up, carrying a large bag of Kentucky fried chicken. She waved to Patti and Joe.

"I can't wait to get my hands on her breasts," joked Billy, eyeing the chicken.

"Grub's up!" yelled Bu, walking over to Cindy and giving her a hug. Benji ran up to Cindy as Patti and Joe emerged from the garage. A small battle followed as everyone grabbed for the food, falling over one another and giggling at their own greediness.

"Beer?" asked Billy.

"In the fridge," said Joe.

"I'll get it," said Billy, jumping up. "Generic?"

"Yeah," answered Patti. "My money, my brand." Billy ran inside, avoiding falling over Gene, who was wrapping his torn tennis shoe in duct tape.

"Speaking of money, what'd we settle for tonight?" asked Gene.

"A hundred twenty-five bucks against a hundred percent of the door," answered Patti.

"In other words, a hundred twenty-five bucks." Gene laughed.

"Plus free drinks and red hots."

"Oh yeah," cheered Bu. "It's gonna be a hot time in Bum Fuck, Egypt." The spaniel ran up to Benji and tried to slurp mashed potatoes from his styrofoam cup. Patti sent the dog running with a slap.

"You gonna baby-sit here tonight, or your place?" Patti asked Cindy.

"Here's easier."

"That way at least one of you has to come home when I do," said Bu.

"I noticed that," Joe joined in. "Can we help if it takes so long to wind down?"

"Bu used to say that," said Cindy.

"I still do," volunteered Bu.

Inside Joe and Patti's kitchen, Billy went to the refrigerator and tucked a six-pack under his arm, but immediately placed it on top of the refrigerator when he noticed the wall phone. He couldn't resist. He picked up the receiver and punched out the numbers for Dial-a-Metal-Riff, a new twenty-four-hour-a-day service. He listened as the phone connected; a short buzz and beep, followed by a blast of Judas Priest. He beat imaginary drums to the guitar riff, and his face lit up with a smile as he lost himself in the steady slam of the beat. The beer could wait.

Saturday night at the Euclid Tavern and the place was packed. After all, this was the last night of the week to party, the last night to score. But getting drunk was the first priority. They said disco never caught on in Cleveland because nobody ever cared about the clothes. That was certainly true of tonight's crowd. The room was wall-to-wall jeans, T-shirts, and logo jackets. Teen conversation mixed with prerecorded music as the girls and guys began an all-too-familiar ritual.

"Come on, let's dance," a girl said to her boyfriend.

"Fuck that. Only black people dance."

"Oh yeah? And what do white people do? Get drunk and fall off their chairs?"

"Yeah, that's right."

Further down the bar, a loaded punk girl approached a guy sitting alone. "Do you want to do the Y dance?"

"What's that?" he asked, putting down his beer bottle.

"Why dance?" She laughed, slipping her hands down his waist and stopping at his crotch.

The stage at the Euclid was minuscule at best: a six-inch platform covered by orange shag. On stage, Joe, Bu, and Billy tuned their instruments. Gene was busy adjusting the mixing board atop a pinball machine—the only available space. He walked back and forth, balancing volume levels. A Barbusters chant went up from the now restless crowd.

"Where is she?" shouted Billy to Joe. All Joe could do was shrug his shoulders helplessly. It was unusual for Patti to be so late.

"What'll we do, Bu?" asked Joe, now becoming angry.

"We start playing, that's what."

"But she should be here by now."

"Well, you sing," Bu said casually.

"No way. I can't sing. I write," Joe answered.

"Start learnin'. Just hit the wa-wa when your voice cracks—like all the biggies do."

"If it's so simple, then *you* sing." Joe really couldn't imagine himself taking over the vocals. The prospect filled him with sudden panic. Bu could sense Joe's fear and reluctance.

"All right," Bu said, "let's do an instrumental 'Night of the Werewolf.' "

"Great," said Joe with a broad smile, feeling immediate relief. Bu picked up his guitar and Joe gave the front two girls pressing up against the stage a wink as the band kicked into Lee Kristofferson's 1959 instrumental, which was a crowd favorite, a guitar show-turn full of cascading riffs. The crowd sent up cheers and started to dance. The sweaty undulating pack had become a single organism. Midway through the instrumental, Joe spotted Patti elbowing her way through the friendly crowd. People on the floor recognized her and waved silent greetings as she got closer to the stage.

Suddenly Joe stopped playing. He just froze. Bu and Billy stopped, turning to each other. The dancers grew silent and still, their eyes glancing from the stage to each other in curiosity. Joe changed his stance, leaned forward into the crowd, and pointed a finger at Patti and sang out the famous first line to "Do Wah Diddy."

Patti stopped in her tracks, threw her hands on her hips, and stared at Joe. The band immediately picked up the shuffling beat. And above the rising music, Joe called out, "It's my sister Patti!"

Patti strutted on stage to cheers and whistles. She and Joe spun their butts toward the crowd, bumped buns, and hugged shoulders. Gene handed Patti her guitar as she grabbed the mike, shouting into the crowds, "All right, *Cleveland*!" The crowd responded, cheering the band on. Patti became totally alive. *This* was what she wanted, needed, and loved. *This* she could respond to. She knew how to handle the crowds. This was a passion she could reach out to and hold on to.

"Are you ready to party?" she screamed with fervor. Cheers and applause swept back over her and the band. Joe looked to Billy at his drums. They traded grins. "Or are you ready to *rock and roll?* Patti urged the crowd to even greater pandemonium. "Well, come *on*!" The crowd screamed as the Barbusters punched into their opening number.

Joe moved slightly behind Patti. She hugged the mike. From behind, Joe could see Patti slip something halfway out of her back pocket for him to see: a chrome toolbox wrench. A chill went through him, but he forced himself back into the music. Only the music. This was not the time to sort out the surge of feelings, the worry and the anger. It saddened him to realize he really wasn't surprised.

6 The following day, Joe awoke with a premonition. He had never believed in such things, so he wrote it off as a bad feeling left over from the day before, the birthday—or D-day, whichever it was. Joe was standing at his spot on the assembly line when the coffee buzzer sounded at 11:00 A.M. Coffee, he thought as he headed toward the bathroom. That's exactly what I've got to get *out* of my system. As he punched the Borax dispenser and leaned forward to wash his face and hands, he noticed two young workers sharing a joint. One of them he recognized as Smitty, a heavyset worker who was about thirty-eight, wearing a green military jacket. Smitty came over to him, and the look on his face was unmistakably unfriendly.

"Hey, Rasnick." The greeting was not cordial.

"Hey, Smitty. What is this? A Vietnam flash-back?" Smitty didn't laugh.

"I got a brother-in-law that lives in Oakhurst. You know that area?"

"A little," Joe lied.

"He got robbed Saturday night. His tools—worth about six hundred bucks."

"That's a fuck all right."

"The fuck is *you* ripped him off. Somebody recognized your car."

"You got a police problem, go to the police. It wasn't me. I was at the Euc all night."

"That hot sister of yours wasn't."

"Ask her."

"I did. She denied everything."

"So tell the cops."

"Listen to me, you faggot rock-and-roller. And listen hard before I pull that earring right out of your fucking ear. I told my brother-in-law I'd take care of it. He doesn't want to go to the cops. He calls the cops he doesn't get his tools back. He needs the tools for his part-time work."

"Take it up with Patti."

"I'll take it up with Patti all right. I'll take it up with her in your driveway. She'll give me her bullshit, then I'll break her arms. Then I'll break her goddamn face. That may give me some satisfaction. But it won't help my brother-in-law and

48

sister. They need money, not satisfaction. You get it, asshole?"

Joe sighed. Of course he got it. He'd been cleaning up after Patti for as long as he could remember, and this was apparently no different. Wearily he said, "Give me twenty-four hours. I'll ask around, maybe I can come up with something."

"Okay, the number is six hundred—"

"I ain't trying to negotiate," Joe broke in.

"And while I'm at it, I might just break both *your* arms. You know, so they can't be fixed. And so you can't play that shit you call music. Now get busy. I'm not the most patient guy." Smitty left the washroom and Joe could feel himself break into a sweat. How long would he have to go on covering his sister's tracks? Maybe one day it would make a good story in *Rolling Stone*. Joe knew the only person he could turn to was his mother, yet how could he expect her to help Patti after the scene at her birthday party. It's only rock and roll, Joe thought, but this part he didn't relish.

At the end of work, Joe went to a pay phone and called his mother. He breathed a silent prayer of relief when she answered. "Ma, I gotta see you. Now."

"Now? Where are you? What's the trouble? Is it Patti? Are you both in any kind of trouble?"

"Ma, please. Just meet me at Randall Park Mall. In front of the 7-eleven."

"Joe baby, you got me real scared. I'm gonna

pray all the way there. If I had a Valium in the house, I'd take it. But they stopped working. Now all I have is a prayer. And don't you laugh!"

"Ma, I love you. And I'm not laughing. Just get on your coat, start praying, and get over here fast."

Randall Park Mall was one of those modern edifices of efficiency that had started spreading over the country almost overnight. The fountains, the ferns, the obsequious and neatly dressed salespeople—and the muzak—all combined to induce shoppers to buy things they didn't need. Overweight couples pushed their way from shop to shop, and screaming children ran free, often losing their parents in the process.

Joan, harried and babbling, met Joe and Benji a few minutes late. "I don't know why I hate driving so much. I used to love— "

Joe broke in. "We got a problem." He let the words sink in before adding, "Me and Patti." There was silence. "We need to borrow some money."

Joan fished absentmindedly in her purse, then pressed a bill into Benji's hand. "Honey," she cooed, "go on over there—see that Walgreen's store? Go over there and get yourself a candy bar." Benji accepted the money happily and scooted away.

Joe continued, "She's in some legal trouble. She

needs six hundred dollars to get out of it. I'll pay you back part each week."

"You should ask your father."

"He'd only ask you."

"Don't make fun of him." There was a flash of anger in her eyes.

"I wasn't."

"He loves you kids."

"Yes." Joe knew this was true, but he couldn't help finding fault in his father's inability to show it.

"Where's Patti?"

"She'd never ask you for help."

"Is she all right?" Her voice quivered with suspicion and fear.

"She's fine."

"We don't have too much money saved . . ."

"I wouldn't ask if there was any other way. I think you know that."

"I could get a clerking job for Christmas. We were thinking of going to Florida. Then somebody else wouldn't get Christmas work."

"Ma, stick to the point."

Suddenly Joan's voice became stern. Joe hadn't heard her like this in ages, and inside he felt some small part of himself tearing apart. "This is the point. Patti gets in trouble, you get in debt. Dad and I don't go to Florida. I work the holidays, another girl loses out on a part-time job, her kids don't get the special presents they wanted—it's all connected. The hardship just gets passed from one person to the next."

"Patti's in trouble. That's the point."

"Why always Patti? What is so special about Patti? We put away money for her to go to college. She drops out, fine. She gets pregnant by some stranger, fine. She won't say who. Fine. She won't talk to her mother. Fine. Whatever Patti wants." Joan reached into her bag for a tissue and wiped her moist eyes.

"Ma. Please."

"I know you know who Benji's father is. You just won't tell me." Her voice was raised and she seemed ready to break, but Joe had to go on.

"I don't know. I don't want to. I'm trying to live in the present."

"Sorry. I'm being stupid. I just have to say these things every now and then." She reached over and took Joe's hand. "Of course I'll get the money. Maybe this will bring us all close again." Joe studied his mother. As grateful as he was that she had come through, he wondered to what degree her feelings were genuine and to what degree they were calculated. He could feel the screws tightening. Was his mother already collecting emotional interest on her loan?

"Don't you think it will? Bring us all closer together?" The pleading in her voice, the sound of futile hope, made it difficult for him to meet her glance. But what else could he say? He reached over and embraced her.

"I'm sure it will," he said with all the emotion going through him. And then the thought, Patti did the crime. I'm doing the time.

The radio broke the silence. Joe turned his sleepy head and dared to look: 6:00 A.M. Hard rock leaped out of the speaker. The window was unshaded, and darkness filled the room. Darkness and rock and roll. Joe's room reflected eclectic taste: an Empire Burlesque poster hung beside one from the Cleveland Art Museum. Magazines and paperbacks were everywhere. Temp lyrics were pinned to the wall. After taking a quick shower, Joe went to his desk drawer. The envelope with the $600 was there. He stuffed it in his inside jacket pocket. As usual, he stopped by Bu's house to pick him up for work. After parking the car and heading for the entrance gate of Marsh Allan Products they noticed a sign posted outside the gate.

ATTENTION: SEASONAL LAYOFFS. ALL TEMPORARY, PART-TIME AND NONSENIORITY EMPLOYEES PLEASE REPORT TO THE EMPLOYMENT OFFICE.

"Damn! exclaimed Bu.

Joe noticed Smitty and handed him the envelope. "This is for your brother-in-law."

"Thanks. Sorry about the layoffs. Sometimes I hear about part-time stuff. House painting. Maybe I can help out."

"Yeah, thanks."

As Joe turned away, Smitty studied him closely. "I like you. You're all right. You got a real family loyalty." He spit on the ground and backed away. "Too bad your sister's not worth it." And he was gone.

The words stung, but Joe didn't make a move. How could he be angry at Smitty for voicing the though that he constantly tried to push from his own mind?

Joe immediately drove back home and went upstairs to Patti's room. Unlike Joe's, Patti's room was entirely undecorated, almost devoid of personality. She rested against the headboard. Patti and Joe shared a liquid breakfast; a can of beer.

"I thought they were doing good at the plant, Joe?"

"They are for somebody else. You know, last hired, blah-blah. Bu had only a month to go to get union. Some banker scratches his ass and we're in the street."

"Maybe there's something else."

"Dream on."

"Well, that settles it." Patti stretched.

"Settles what? You going back to sleep?" He looked at her with disgust.

"Settles that we're going on the road. We got a rep. We can get booked into bars in Erie, Akron, Mansfield. You got no job, Bu's got no job—let's get serious."

Joe immediately felt himself energized. "We got material."

"We got a Peavy."

"Bongo Boy?"

"The youngest roadie!"

Now there were things to get done in preparation for the adventure that awaited them on the road. The first was a yard sale at Joe and Patti's house. The yard had been turned into a miscellany of used equipment and clothes. The next stop was a car lot, where Joe and Bu bartered with a car salesman over a used van. Joe hyped the Nova and Bu's motorcycle and traded them both for a beat-up Econoline stretch van.

The last stop was the most difficult. Saying good-bye to Benjamin and Joan Rasnick was not going to be easy. The Econoline pulled up to the Rasnick's home early the next morning. Joe and Patti and Benji found Joan and Benjamin waiting for them on the front porch.

"Coffee's all ready, and I've packed some sandwiches for the trip. You'll need them. I remember how hungry you used to get on long drives."

They all sat around the dining-room table drinking coffee while Joan busied herself making large portions of bacon and eggs. "Oh, Ma, that's more than enough. We'll never get on the road," Joe said impatiently.

"Now, now, let me have my enjoyment of seeing you off with a good meal. I've checked ahead with Triple A and they assure me that the roads are all clear and good weather is expected. I used the itinerary you gave me." Patti and Joe smiled at her concern.

"And you be sure to stay in touch. Let us know how you're doing," Ben uncharacteristically chimed in.

"I was at church first thing this morning. Don't joke about it either. I asked for your safety and for success for you too." Joe got up and embraced his mother, whose eyes had started to moisten.

Ben Rasnick stood up and picked up Benji. "Little fella, I may miss you most of all. You may have noticed through the years, I'm not big on words or emotion. But I hope for the best, that along the way you find what makes you happy. And never be afraid to come back if you want to. Your grandmother and I have what you might call some good luck presents for your trip. How are you at giving hugs?" The family joined together in a long silent embrace, and then Patti and Joe and Benji made their way to the Econoline. They waved and waved as the white van sped away. Only then did Patti and Joe open their gifts. In their father's envelope was a crisp new hundred-dollar bill. Inside their mother's package was the family Bible, which she had inscribed on the front page. "Sometimes help can come from places you never expect. I wanted this to be with you. It goes with generations of love."

Patti stared grimly at the thick book on her lap. It was just like her mother to get the last little jab in when everything was going well. Wouldn't the woman ever learn? When would she stop thinking of Patti's entire life as a problem? It pained her to know that her mother cared, yet expressed her caring in a way that made Patti angry.

Patti and Joe glanced at each other, neither sure of what to say or how to say it. So they turned on the radio, and the voice of Kid Leo filled the van. "Cleveland Rocks! Cleveland Rocks!" And now they were off to become part of it.

The white van sped through an afternoon drizzle toward Pennsylvania. In the distance, Lake Erie blended into the overcast horizon. This first part of the trip had been exhilarating. The group split the driving, and inventing ways to pass the time hadn't proved difficult at all. They sang along with songs on the radio, and even resorted to games like geography from long ago. Even Benji seemed to be caught up in the excitement of traveling to an unknown destination.

It was early evening when they arrived at the Emergency Room, a local club like many others across the country. It wasn't the big time, but it was a chance. The Emergency Room was part of an Erie shopping center. The once-thriving strip was now just another half-occupied urban eyesore. Gene, Billy, and Bu carried primerblack JBLs out of the van.

Inside the club, Patti and Joe crowded around the manager, a forty-year-old man called Mason. He was an overweight, long-haired hippie throwback who wore extra-large rock-and-roll T-shirts, and even then they were too small to cover his huge stomach, which showed that too much free beer had taken its toll.

"I didn't know if you'd make it," joked Mason.

"What do you mean?" Patti shot back. "We're a road band now."

"So you told me," said Mason, without enthusiasm.

Joe figured he'd better assert himself quickly. "Two hundred twenty-five against three, fifty percent of the door. Two sets, nine forty-five to two. Drinks half price."

"Wait a sec. Who've you been talking to? Bill Graham? Where'd you get those numbers? I never guaranteed more than one seventy-five to a band without an album."

Patti jabbed her fingers into Mason's stomach. "That's what you quoted on the phone. The Frenchmen got two-fifty here."

"I don't care what I said on the phone. Besides, the Frenchmen are hot poo here."

"So are we," Patti said seductively, her hand now gently patting Mason's stomach. She thought she might throw up.

"You may be hot poo in Cleveland, but you're warm snot here."

"Hey, let's not get nasty. I know the sixties must have been rough," Joe groaned.

"O.K., O.K. One seventy-five. But drinks half price for the band only."

"But we got only *one* roadie," Joe protested.

"He pays full. House policy. Take it or leave it." They had no choice. They needed the dough, and they needed the practice.

"O.K. But Patti and Benji get a free room next door; the rest of us will crash in the van. Well, let's get ready. If you can't lower heaven, raise hell!"

The show was a mixed success at best. Just as it did at most clubs, the crowd only warmed to cover versions of past hits. But the Barbusters were troopers. They played and sang their hearts out and never relented in their attempt to spark the lukewarm crowd's interest. A couple of hitter types even made their way backstage after the show to tell Patti how much they liked her songs. Patti only briefly acknowledged their compliments.

"Listen guys, I'm glad you dug us. But we hit the road again tomorrow, and we've got to get some shuteye. So if you'll be good enough to excuse us, we gotta split now. Maybe one day you'll buy our records." The two guys, put off, quickly left the dressing room.

"Gee, Patti. You coulda been a little more friendly."

"Get this, brother. I know a line when I hear one. All they liked was my ass. And my ass is real tired now. If you want to, *you* screw him!"

Joe knew Patti's moods and there was no sense in causing a scene now. Tomorrow was another long drive, and another club. What they needed now was sleep.

7   Just as love can turn to hate, so Joe discovered that anticipation and excitement can turn to boredom and frustration. To the outsider, the thought of traveling from rock club to rock club and playing to new audiences may seem thrilling, but the Barbusters were starting to feel otherwise. Even Benji was beginning to show the frustration the others were feeling. His mood was irritable, and it was clear he missed the stability of a "real" home. A new game the group played in the van as they drove day after day was listing the things they liked *least*.

"Hamburgers!" offered Bu.

"*Death*burgers, you mean." Patti laughed.

"Traveling from town to town."

"Not getting enough sleep."

"Not getting any sex," Joe retorted.

"Not getting enough money."

"Not getting enough encores."

"Smoking more and enjoying it less," said Patti, lighting a Merit 100, which she had taken to calling DeMerits. She had convinced herself that switching from Marlboros would protect her health.

Six months had passed, and the winter was still upon them. That night's gig was at the Rathskeller in Kalamazoo, Michigan, a suburban club between Shakey's and Kentucky Fried. The club was on a four-lane running from Western Michigan University. The marquee advertised: FRI-SAT: FROM CLEVELAND—THE BARBUSTERS. Snow had been plowed into three-foot banks alongside the highway. Cars idled in the crowded parking lot; exhaust smoke billowed past the club. Four sophomores jumped from their car, slapping the cold away and high-stepping through the snow. The winter wind sliced through them, sending chills up their spines. They laughed and rough-housed as they approached the club. When they opened the door, a forcefield of smoke, noise, and steam hit the students. The impact was electric, and Alan, one of the sophomores, had to strain to see through his steamy glasses.

On stage, the Barbusters were going full blast. Joe finished a power chord as Pattie belted out the vocal, bouncing the balls of her feet to the beat.

She was wearing harlequin shades and a Bundeswehr tanktop. They were debuting a new song, a hard 4/4 Dave Edmunds-style rocker. Patti was right, one hour like this made up for the other twenty-three. On the dance floor, the sophomores mixed with preppies and townies. All across the room, horny undergrads were getting drunk, screaming for women and acting stupid.

The club had a novelty device none of the Barbusters had ever seen before. For a quarter, patrons could test their sobriety on a wall-mounted "Breathalyzer." Students waited in an unsteady line, each hoping to be the most drunk.

"Hey, stupid," one student called another.

"My name ain't stupid. It's Bob."

"That may be, but I call them as I see them!"

Watching from the edge of the stage was Sean, twenty, Patti's loser boyfriend, a recent acquisition. At first glance, he was sexy and cool. A closer look revealed that he was as disposable as Kleenex. But Patti wasn't looking at him now. She was hot tonight, and all alone, lost in a world of her own, singing of work and freedom. Joe kept glancing at her, trying his best to pick up her incredible energy, and the attempt was successful. He loved seeing his sister like this. More than anything, he knew this was her life, and he could never imagine her doing anything else.

At the end of the gig, the band packed into the van and pulled into the parking lot of the Red

Roof Inn. Places like this were high on the list of things the group liked least. And the van was starting to show its wear: dirty snow and rock salt streaked its exterior. They were now on the outskirts of Flint, but they could have been anywhere. Everything had started looking the same. And one thing never changed: the incredible exhaustion the band felt as they fell into their beds, often too tired to talk or watch the late night movies they automatically switched the television dials to find.

The peculiar sound of cartoon voices suddenly woke Joe. At first, he figured he was having a junk food-inspired dream, but as his eyes fully opened, he saw Sean sitting with Benji watching cartoons. Joe was pissed at Sean, the freeloader who vied for Patti and Benji's attention.

"What the fuck's going on here?" Joe demanded. He couldn't imagine why Sean was in the room Joe shared with Bu, and why Benji was in there too.

"Don't you think you should watch your language in front of the kid?" asked Sean, without much interest. He was rolling joints, one of which he had just lit.

"Answer my question," Joe replied angrily.

"I couldn't sleep, and Benji woke up to take a piss. I didn't want to wake Patti, so I asked Benji if he wanted to come in here and catch the cartoons. Some of my favorites are on in the morning." Joe jumped out of bed and turned the television off, which only made Benji start to cry. Sean held him. "Don't cry, Benji boy. Your uncle seems to be in a bad mood this morning." This was all Joe needed—having to defend himself to Benji. Just then there was a sharp knock at the door, and Patti walked into the room yawning. She was wearing underwear and a T-shirt.

"I was fast asleep, and your boyfriend here just decided to let himself in my room with Benji to turn on my TV." But Patti failed to recognize Joe's reason for being upset.

"Don't be so touchy. Anyway, I'm starved. Let's go buy some food." With those words, the decision was immediately made to travel to the nearby "Food and Stuff" supermarket. "Let's all hit the showers and split."

Joe, Patti, and Sean pushed their shopping cart through the well-lit aisles with Benji riding in the cart. Patti held on to Sean's arm as Joe picked out a box of detergent.

The wear of the last six months showed on their faces. Benji too seem disoriented. Joe glanced at Sean, still pissed. Just another emotion I have to swallow, he thought.

"Four days, one gig," said Patti. "Seems like home."

"Do we need softener?" asked Joe.

"No."

"Get some hash and eggs," Joe told Sean, "and some bleach." Sean didn't respond. "Get some bleach, please," he repeated.

"Huh?" Sean seemed terribly uninterested.

"Bleach. B-L-E-A-C-H!" Joe was getting snotty. "Put it in the cart. Please."

"My name's Sean."

"Sean, please. I try not to ask too much of you. I know how hard it is hanging around like a lapdog."

"Stop it," ordered Patti. "Just back off, Joey. Take the scenic route." Joe shrugged an apology.

"It's O.K." Sean's voice had turned sincere.

Joe did a double take—is this guy snide or just dumb? Joe settled on dumb.

"I shoulda called home weeks ago. I'll do it now. Anything you want to say?" Joe asked Patti.

"No, nothing, not a thing."

Joe wasn't surprised. He waved to Benji as he turned to the aisle. Finding a pay phone, Joe placed a collect call. He looked around as the call went through. His side of the conversation consisted mostly of nods and noncommittal acknowledgments— "Yes," "No," "Soon," and "Fine." He hung up and set off to find the others. Turning a corner, Joe saw them at the meat counter and stopped dead in his tracks. Patti and Sean, using Benji as a decoy, were tucking steaks into their waistbands. Sean entertained Benji with comic expressions as he slipped a small steak under the child's sweatshirt. They moved down the aisle. Joe managed to compose himself.

"You call?" Patti asked, seeing Joe.

"Yeah, Mom was sick for a couple of days but's all right now. They canceled Florida."

"And Dad?"

"You know. Got on the phone. Asked how we were. I said fine. He said something about the weather and gave the phone back to Mom." They headed toward the checkout counters. "You get the hash?" asked Joe.

"It's there." Patti pointed. "You need a haircut, brother. I'll cut it." She looked closer. "You're getting gray."

"I am not!"

"I guess not," Patti agreed as she touched his hair. Patti and Sean unloaded the cart, each careful not to bend too far. Patti studied Joe's hair from one angle, then another. "Must just be some dust or powder." Now Joe was being used as the decoy; he knew it and he was pissed. The checkout girl rang up their groceries.

Joe looked Patti in the eye. "Isn't there something else you forgot?" His voice was as cold and steely as his gaze.

"No. What?" Joe examined Patti's face for a trace of guilt or anxiety, but there was none.

Benji touched his stomach. "Mom, it's cold," he complained.

"You're fine, Benji." And then to Sean, "Why

67

don't you warm up the van?" And to Benji, "You just be quiet." Sean exited as the checkout girl totaled the bill: $38.19. Joe hesitated, then pulled out his money. Benji, frightened, looked at Joe.

When the van pulled outside the one-story row of rooms of the Red Roof Inn, snow was falling. Inside the room, band instruments and equipment were stacked everywhere. Billy and Gene sat on one double bed, while Bu played with Benji on the other. Billy drank a beer as he watched the silent TV. Gene read *Ripley's Believe It or Not*.

Patti waited on food over a hot plate. Killing time, she improvised "The Patty Duke Show" theme to a rock beat. Billy and Bu joined in. Joe, in a chair, went over the expenses.

"Here's what she wrote. It ain't much. Slow week. Three travel days plus the flat. We grossed eight-fifty. Fifty for a van payment. Eighty, gas. Twenty-five, bar fund. Thirty for the tire. One-ten for groceries; twenty-five, Chinese dinner. That leaves two-eighty, or fifty-six dollars each." Joe distributed the money. Each counted his share and pocketed it.

Bu stood up, pulled on his down jacket, and gloves. "I'm gonna call my baby. Maybe we can talk about what she wants for Christmas."

"Is that a complaint?" Joe asked.

"No, not really."

"Tell Cindy to say hello to my parents?" Billy asked.

"Mine too," echoed Gene.

"Will do," promised Bu.

"Come back soon," Patti said, blowing Bu a kiss. A winter breeze swirled through the room as he left.

"Winter's a bitch," said Joe. "Summer everybody can spread out. Sleep in the van, or the grass."

"I think this is the greatest book ever written," said Gene, not really listening to Joe.

"What is it?" Billy asked.

Believe It or Not.

"Get off it," chided Billy.

"I'm serious, man. You just think about it."

"What's with the franks, Patti? I'm hungry," complained Billy. Patti did a theatrical turn.

"No 'Injun dogs' tonight. I got a special surprise." She stuck her head out the door, calling to Sean. The van door slammed. Sean entered, proudly carrying the three stolen steaks. He handed them to Patti and she held them up. "A special treat. I've been saving up. It's a thank-you." Gene and Billy applauded. Joe just stared at Patti. Sean bent down to pick up Benji.

"What'ya think, Benji, you little secret weapon?" Sean asked.

Joe's voice filled with ice and anger. "Don't touch him! Don't you ever touch him." Patti started to protest. "You shut up!" Joe shouted at her.

"What?" Patti asked in disbelief.

"You're such a low-life bitch, Patti."

"What is this?" She pretended confusion.

"You've done some low shit, but this tops it." Joe stood and faced Sean. "And you, loser, better get your loser ass out of here as fast as your loser legs can take you. I've seen just about enough of you fucking around my family. Get going and don't stop. You're interferin' with our conversation."

Sean, trembling, turned to Patti, but found no support there. He immediately headed out. Just as Joe had suspected, the boy's spine was made of mush. Patti didn't react. She had never really deceived herself; she didn't care much for him anyway. But just then Joe turned his anger to Patti.

"Do what you want with your life, but Benji ain't just yours. He's mine and Mom and Dad's and his own too."

Patti dropped the steaks. "What bullshit is this?"

"You gotta use a four-year-old to boost steaks from the supermarket?"

"I don't know what you're talking about. I bought those steaks."

Joe was repulsed by Patti's obvious lie. "Shut your lying mouth."

Patti counterattacked. "You got a real attitude, little brother. Maybe we ought to start a band just for you. Call it 'the "Attitudes.' " This was start-

ing to get thick. Gene buried his head in a pillow.
Billy stood up.

"I gotta take a piss."

"Take Benji with you?" asked Joe. "Go on, son."
Benji walked over to Billy; they went into the
bathroom.

Patti turned back to Joe. "Excuse me. I didn't
know you were above stealing food to eat. You
get converted?"

"What you gonna do next? Turn him out? I
hear there's big bucks in child porn."

Patti went white; her face blank, her voice calm.
"You bastard. You're even worse than the rest of
them." She strode out of the room, not bothering
to take her jacket. Gene dared to peek from under
his pillow. Bu ran out after Patti and found her in
a neighborhood Flint bar. A half-dozen regulars
sat along the bar. The tables and stage were empty.
Patti stood in the corner, practicing guitar chords.
As Bu walked over to say something, jukebox
music drowned out their conversation. Together,
they drove back to the motel and walked to the
room.

"Benji," Patti called out. She checked the closet,
then looked under the bed. Billy was watching
silent TV from the other bed. Patti turned to him.

"They split, Billy said without looking.

Patti felt all emotion drain. "What now?" she
asked herself. "Shit!"

*   *   *

Patti immediately left the Red Roof Inn and made her way back home. The driveway hadn't been shoveled; snow covered the yard, sidewalk and steps. The house was dark. Patti banged on the screen door. No answer. Frantic now, she went to her parents' house. The van was parked on the freshly shoveled drive, and a Christmas wreath adorned the door. Patti rang the bell, and almost instantly Joe cracked open the storm door. He wore a faded flannel shirt and jeans.

"Let me in," Patti demanded. "Where's Benji?" Her voice was filled with worry and anger. Joe didn't answer. "Look, I'm sorry. Let me in. It's cold out here."

Without enthusiasm, Joe opened the door for her. Patti entered and stomped snow from her boots and removed her jacket. A Christmas tree stood decorated in the living room.

"Where's Benji?" Patti repeated impatiently.

"He's with Mom," Joe told her, his voice devoid of emotion.

"Would you get him?"

"You go. They're in the den. I didn't tell her a thing." Patti draped her motorcycle jacket over a chair and headed toward the den, followed by Joe. A daytime soap echoed from the family room. Joe decided to wait in the kitchen while Patti entered the den. Benji and Joan looked up as she entered. Benji ran to her and Patti knelt to embrace him.

"Hi Mom," Patti greeted Joan. Joan said nothing. The tension was building. Patti turned to her mother. Her voice was brittle. "What is it now? I mean, you usually have so much to say." Patti's tone frightened Benji, and he instinctively returned to his grandmother.

"Benji already said enough," Joan explained as she held her hands out to Benji.

"Said enough what?" Patti tried to remain strong in the face of the impending confrontation.

"You know—but maybe you should hear it from a four-year-old's point of view. Being lugged around from place to place in a van. Waking up with no one to talk to. What do you think he is, a suitcase?"

"I'm leaving. Let's go, Benji." Benji didn't budge.

"Reverend Ansley says you should speak to a counselor. I want you to speak to him."

Patti was incredulous. "You took *my* problems to a minister? How could you? What does he have to do with anything?"

Joe, who had been listening from the kitchen, sighed.

Joan's voice became sterner. "It's not going to be so easy this time. You're going to have to prove yourself. From what I see, you're no fit mother—or wife, or sister, or—"

"I *am* Benji's mother—and since when are you an authority on fit mothers?" Patti felt a surge of regret the moment she spoke, but she couldn't control herself. And she hated others trying to control her. Joe walked in to intervene, and took Patti's arm.

"C'mon, sis. You're tired. You look damn near dead. This can wait. Get some rest."

"I won't stay in this house."

"Let's go downstairs and have a beer. C'mon." He edged a reluctant Patti out the door. Benji stayed with his grandmother. Joe took Patti to the basement study, where she curled up on a worn sofa in the study, an unfinished room lined with religious books. A humidifier hummed beside an old desk. Joe entered the room with two beers, unsnapped them, and wiped the foam on his jeans. He handed Patti a beer and sat beside her. Even with what they had been through, Joe still felt great affection for Patti.

"You want a neck massage?" Patti shook her head and took a swig of beer.

Silence settled in. Patti spoke, almost to herself. "Benji can't stay here. Not with her. I really love Benji, you know."

"I know," said Joe, deeply moved by his sister.

"I admit I ain't been the best mother. That thing in Michigan was real stupid. Sorry." Another period of silence followed. Patti was in a reflective mood, a mood that didn't come upon her often. "I could have had an abortion. Mom would never have found out. Sometimes I wonder what would have happened if I had—I'm a damn good singer, Joey. That's all I seem to really know."

"You are. Damn good."

"Then I look at Benji and get so full of feelings and just want to hit myself for feeling that way. I was so young. I wanted something that was *mine*, something she had no part of. I was so sick of this house, this furniture, those calendars." She pointed to an extremely tacky fish mounted on the wall behind them. "This fish—some reasons, huh? I thought a baby could change everything. Where were you then?"

Lightly, Joe resounded, "Mom asked me to pray for you so I asked God: Make Mom leave you alone."

"So much for prayer." Patti laughed. And then, after a pause, "You'd be surprised if you knew who the father was."

Joe had taken aback. "You said you didn't know."

Patti smirked; neither believed this convenient falsehood. "It was somebody Mom respected—an 'older' man, like maybe thirty—from the church. That woulda killed her. But I still wouldn't tell. I couldn't give her that control over me."

"Benji's *your* son. Let it go at that."

Patti stood up and started punching the air. Maybe that would calm her. She had once read somewhere that it would.

"I just get so angry. Everybody's always getting

on ya, telling you what to do, what to be. You're in an open coffin. If you show any emotion, smile, even give 'em that much . . ." Patti fell back on the sofa. "Wham! Down comes the lid. We gotta stick together."

Joe walked over to the shelves and tried to lighten the mood. "Like all these books. Mom bought them all because she wanted Dad to be a minister. But he couldn't read them. They were over his head. They were over *her* head. I'd sit down here for hours. She was so proud. Told all her friends. But then she found out I was reading Foxe's martyr book, all the persecutions, tortures of the early Christians."

Patti laughed. "Innocent maidens raped by evil Rome."

"That was the end of my religious training."

"I was thinking." Patti's rage had vanished, replaced by a slight smile and gleaming eyes.

"What?"

"The band sucks. Got no getup, no punch. We gotta tighten up when we get back on the road. We gotta attack, fist in the face. Reverb, staccato repeats, metal riffs. Further out."

Joe took another beer. "Metal? I wasn't even a metal head when everybody else was a metal head."

"Not just metal. A new sound, like—techno-pop metal. Pure noise. Blast through the walls. You can play it and the lyrics are no problem."

"Metal ain't got lyrics."

Flirty, Patti said, "That's what I mean. What'ya think?" Joe didn't care much for metal. All he could do was shrug. "Huh?" Patti asked.

Reluctantly, Joe said, "Okay."

"Okay what?"

"Okay, I'm thinking about it." Joe had a lot to think about. Aside from Patti and their parents, Joe wished he felt as confident as Patti about the band, their sound, and whether real success was waiting for them.

8 Later that week, Joe and some of the Barbusters went to the Cleveland Music Hall. Joe had a date named Crystal, a busty blond airhead. The Cleveland Music Hall was a municipal fortress overlooking Lake Erie. Built in 1928 as a showcase for art, it now featured wrestling matches, recreational-vehicle conventions, and rock and roll. It was doubtful that the hall's builders could have anticipated their edifice of culture as a place that would one day gather much of its revenue from screaming teenagers.

A nationally known group was headlining, wailing on stage. The teenage crowd was on its feet, fists raised high in a ritual gesture of support. Bu and Cindy stood next to Joe and Crystal. They cheered, often singing along.

At intermission, Bu and Joe squeezed through the rowdy crowd. Cindy and Crystal followed. They passed a row of tables as high-schoolers hawked rock wares: T-shirts, posters, photo albums. The marble lobby pounded with teen energy. Joe and Bu collected beers and distributed them. They continued toward the rest rooms.

"Good crowd," noted Joe, standing at a urinal.

"Good as tits," joked Bu, next to him. He turned to Joe on his other side and whispered, "Where'd you meet Miss West Virginia?"

"Not bad, huh? Checked my brain at the door, I guess."

"Right next to my self-respect. All set she's been banging me with those bazookas. Up, down . . ." He rubbed his crotch. "Cindy's gonna get one hell of a fuck out of this." Bu then changed the subject. "Look, they're rehiring at the plant. I got notified because of my time. What do you think?"

"What about the Barbusters?"

"To tell you the truth, I got approached by a lounge act in Maple Heights, the No Exits. Guaranteed four hundred for Friday and Saturday."

Joe was appalled. "Jesus, Bu, they're a Top-40 band. You might as well be working in a factory."

"I'm gonna do that too. My baby ran up a lotta bills when we were on the road. We need money."

"But Top 40?"

Bu corrected him with a smile. "Easy listening."

"Oh my God." Joe sighed.

"Who's talking Top 40? You're lead guitar. You think these kids give a damn who plays bass? I just stand in the back there . . . You don't even see the bass players face on MTV . . . more like his fingers." He quickly switched topics again. "It's time I reminded Cindy what my face looks like. I ain't gonna fuck up this marriage. It's not like the Barbusters were exactly going anywhere."

"What about the others?"

"I heard Billy's looking for a better gig. Gene's old man's trying to get him day work. I could mention you to the No Exits."

"No, for me it's the Barbusters or nothing. But maybe I should put my name in at the plant."

"I'm way ahead of you. I put it in with mine."

After the concert, Joe and Crystal returned to Joe and Patti's house, where a surprise awaited Joe. Patti had packed their clothes and stacked the suitcases with the band equipment. Joe stopped short. Crystal, of course, didn't realize something was amiss.

Patti entered, dressed in black slacks and leather. "Great, you're here," she said, seeing Joe.

"What's going on?" Joe asked, confused.

Crystal extended her hand. "I'm Chris. Crystal,

really." Patti seemed to ignore the greeting. She was too enthusiastic to get on with her explanation.

"I've been on the phone all night. There was an ad in *Scene:* a Columbus metal group needs a girl to front for them. They're a guitar short too—maybe we could talk Bu in too. They already know us. We audition tomorrow, and if it works out, we could be gigging in three weeks. They're ragged, but you and me, we'll put the screws to 'em."

Joe tried to remain calm. There goes Patti again, he thought. Total control. "What group is this?"

"The Hunzz. H-U-N-Z-Z."

Crystal jumped into the conversation. "Ick. I saw them. They're all greasy with stringy red hair and their chests open. It's like they try not to get tan."

"That's them," Patti said, clearly repulsed by this squeaky-clean girl. She looked at Joe. "You've outdone yourself." Joe ignored Patti's remark. He felt that she had little room to comment on his girlfriends when she hung out with slime like Sean. At least Crystal *looked* respectable.

"If I was you, I'd give some thought to unpacking."

"If I was you, I'd mind my own business—and start working your riffs," she countered.

"This is *my* business. I'm not going."

Crystal, confused, turned to Joe. Patti, in turn, turned on the helpless teen.

"And what did he tell you, Chris? Did he tell

Michael J. Fox stars as Joe Rasnik, a young man struggling to keep his drifting family together as he and his sister try to make it in the world of rock and roll.

Joe and his sister Patti *(Joan Jett)*, leaders of The Barbusters, plan a robbery so they can buy equipment for the band.

While Joe lectures Patti and her loser boyfriend Sean *(Jerry Gideon)*, Patti uses her son Benji *(Billy Sullivan)* as a decoy for shoplifting.

Endless hours of grinding work at a metal factory fill Joe's days, but his creative drive is unleashed at night with The Barbusters.

With the musical influences of Patti and Joe, Benji demonstrates early signs of rock-and-roll talent.

The Barbusters make last minute plans before going on the road.

Torn between her roles as mother and rock performer, Patti is forced to take Benji on the road.

Yet another worry for Joe is his mother Joan *(Gena Rowlands)*, who desperately wants to strengthen the family ties as her health declines.

"She's trying to destroy us," Patti warns of their mother. "Music is all that matters."

Patti shares a dance with Gene *(Michael Dolan)*, the band's roadie.

After leaving The Barbusters, Patti joins a heavy metal group called The Hunzz.

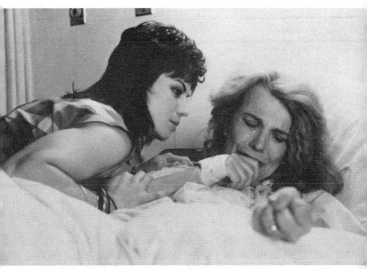

A secret is revealed as Joan lies on her deathbed.

"What will I do now?" Joe's father *(Harry Dean Stanton)* wonders in the face of his family's tragedy.

At Joan's funeral, Bu Montgomery *(Michael McKean)* asks Joe to rejoin The Barbusters.

Brother and sister are reunited—on and off stage.

you about his sensitive soul? Did he get around to his suicidal fantasies—that's a good come-on. Or did he just say he liked your personality. Your 'pep'? Crystal, I'm a fraid it's curfew time." Crystal turned to Joe but she no longer existed for him.

Crystal felt lost. "I don't have a ride home."

"Boo!" Patti shouted. It worked. Crystal fled, slamming the door.

"Patti, I ain't goin', and Bu ain't goin—and you ain't goin'!" Joe said defiantly.

"Well, well, they finally got to you. Welcome to the lineup. Mom, Reverend Ansley, the whole gang. Everybody telling Patti what she can do. Aren't you a little ashamed? There's a mirror in the john if you dare to look at it."

Joe, feeling chastised, backed off. "What about Benji?"

"Already packed."

"Go—with my blessing—"

"I will—"

"Blow out the fucking walls." Joe armed himself with all his nerve for what was next. "But you ain't taking Bongo. He ain't going on the road again. Not with some metal band."

"He's my son, remember?"

"He's still staying here."

"With you?"

"Um-hmm."

"And with Mom?"

"If necessary."

"What's your problem? You want to be so good someday you never have to shit? Benji comes with me. And that's final!" Joe flopped a Smurfs suitcase on the sofa and opened it. "He ain't staying with her!" Patti screamed. Joe continued to toss out pint-size clothes.

"Patti, he ain't going on the road!"

"Well, I am, and you or nobody else can stop me."

"Patti, just go. Please go!" Patti tried to repack Benji's clothes.

"A mother has rights! Any court will tell you that!" They started to struggle over a pair of tiny jeans.

"I don't need no court! Leave if you want, but Benji's staying!" Patti pushed Joe, and Joe pushed her back with even greater force. Furious, she picked up a guitar stand and cracked him across the back. The sound of the whack filled the room. Joe winced, and instinctivley spun around and smacked Patti in the face. She howled as blood started coming from her nose. They both froze, shaking, terrified. Their eyes were wide open. They had never been this far. Both thought, What happens next? Neither of them knew.

Benji, crying and sleepy, started walking down the stairs. "Mom?" he asked. Joe ran to Benji and swept him up, pressing the boy's face against his chest.

"Bongo, don't cry. It's all right." Joe looked at Patti. "We both love you." He carried Benji out the door, not daring to look back. My God, what comes next? Joe thought. What can come next?

Exhausted, Joe sat with Bu and Cindy in their living room. He had gone there to drop Benji off for the evening. Tomorrow morning, Joe would take him to his folks' house. He didn't relish the explanations he'd make to them, nor the "I told you so's" he'd hear. Again, he'd have to find a way to defend Patti. But right now he couldn't think about that. He'd go over Patti's "defense list" in the morning. Now he just wanted company, caffeine, and beer—the nutrients of the world's fledgling rock stars.

"You'll see, it won't last. It will be one of Patti's quicker phases," Cindy said as she gently held Joe's hand.

"I guess we'll be toiling together at the factory, old pal," Joe said as he exhaled cigarette smoke.

"Great!" said Bu, with real enthusiasm.

And why not? Misery loves company, Joe thought to himself.

"I'll leave a pillow and blanket on the couch, but I've got to get to bed." Cindy stood up and gave Joe a kiss on the forehead before leaving the room.

"I think I'll join her," said Bu. He finished off

his can of beer. "You want to take a couple of days off, or just start right in with me?"

"What's the sense of postponing the pain? And what would I do with time off? No, I'll start with you, buddy. You know, together wherever we go."

Long after Bu and Cindy had gone to sleep, Joe lay awake. He couldn't stop the motors of his mind racing after his body had given in to defeat. And he was still angry with Patti. Patti. So much of his life revolved around her.

When they were just kids growing up together, Joe remembered it was Patti who had all the friends. And Joe remembered how happy he was when Patti allowed him to join her and some of her friends when they went to the movies. He enjoyed eavesdropping on their girl talk, listening to their secret desires about older boys at school. In high school, many of those older boys sought Joe out, but only to find out if he would put in a good word for them with his older sister.

But then came music! Patti had been first there too, bringing home records and fan magazines. They would put a whole stack of singles on, and Patti would lip-sync the vocals. She would finally make them her own, singing above the recorded voices and acting out dance steps. As Joe watched her in awe, he began to accompany her with his imaginary guitar. And then he knew he would have to save his money, take part-time jobs, and wait until he could afford a real guitar. Then he could really belong!

Joe remembered vividly the night Patti came home from a school dance crying. She had been to a dance with Vinny, a guy at school with a bad reputation. He was her boyfriend, at least until that night. Joe walked into her bedroom and found her sitting on the bed drying her eyes with a handful of Kleenex. Vinny had seen another girl at the dance, a blonde from a good family, a girl who had never even acknowledged him. But that night they had danced together, and Vinny told Patti he wouldn't be taking her home.

Joe was confused. How could anyone drop his sister? Joe thought she was the best thing going. None of the girls he had taken out could compare to her. And he felt more relaxed with her. Other girls gave him a tough time. They all wanted to be his friend. They "liked" him, but not in "that" way. Joe felt he didn't have it in him to be aggressive enough. His attempt at being macho just didn't work somehow. He couldn't imagine what it would take to get himself laid.

But the night that Patti came home from the dance alone, she had suggested to him that they start a band. Joe wondered whether or not she was doing this to somehow spite Vinny, trying to find some really far-out way to make him jealous, or at least take notice of just how hot and special she was. But Joe hadn't questioned her motives.

A band with Patti! Joe and Patti Rasnick making rock and roll! Joe felt a sudden warm rush of confidence he had never known before. It felt right. It felt good. Joe and Patti in a band!

Remembering that happy time, Joe finally fell asleep.

The next morning, Patti rushed through the task of transforming herself into a heavy-metal contender. She teased her hair up and out with a brush; when that wasn't enough, she pulled it further and further out and up. Before starting her makeup, she went to her album collection for inspiration and tossed records all over the room in search of something by Bon Jovi, but finally had to settle for Quiet Riot. She hurriedly put the album on the turntable and turned the volume all the way up. After lighting a cigarette, she went to her full-length mirror and practiced some poses and mean looks. Now it was time for makeup. She opened her bureau drawer, and not immediately finding what she was looking for, she pulled the entire drawer out and emptied its contents on her bed. Her hands raced through a pile of tubes and containers until she found some green eye shadow. That was what she needed: green eye shadow. Lots of it.

The bar where the audition was held was no different from any other bar. The walls were covered with graffiti. The five members of the Hunzz were sitting around, and when Patti walked in, they studied her carefully. Her piecemeal metal melange of motorcycle jacket and bicycle-chain necklace was good enough for starters. The group wore open leather vests, spiked belts and bracelets, and their pants were slung to the pubic area. Under the white light, devoid of makeup, their faces were ordinary and unattractive, and between them, they covered the whole gamut of possible dermatological ailments. No time was spent on social amenities. They just got up on stage and started playing. Unaided, Patti jumped onto the stage, leaned into the mike, and started singing. The transformation from rock and roll to metal was easy for her voice to make. She radiated, she felt confident and relaxed and free. And the Hunzz found their front girl.

The tour was to start immediately. There would be no time for good-byes or phone calls to friends. That was fine with Patti. She didn't feel like dealing with her family. That was the past. Patti welcomed the race away from that and into the future.

Back at home, Patti kept throwing clothes into a small piece of luggage. Her choices were indiscriminate, and she only stopped when the suitcase was full. As she was closing the lock, she noticed the framed picture on her night table, a photo of her with Benji and Joe. In the rush of the day, she hadn't let herself think about them at all. She picked it up and felt a surge of sadness wash over her. She wished she hadn't seen the damned picture, but she had. This was no time for sentiment. Impatient now, she threw open the luggage and tossed the picture inside. It landed faceup. "Wish me luck," she said to it, and just as quickly she snapped the bag closed.

She was on her way.

9 During the winter and fall, Joe came to accept the fact that nobody really missed the Barbusters. When a band has never made a record and suddenly breaks up, it becomes a lazy and distant memory. Such was a fact of rock and roll.

Occasionally, Joe read small items about the Hunzz. Once he even saw a picture of the band in a local paper. Patti looked dark and menacing, her face caught at a moment when she looked as if she were growling. Joe decided not to show Benji the picture. Benji asked less and less for Patti. Joe didn't think of this as cruel. Forgetting was a definite blessing reserved for infants. Anyway, Benji seemed happy enough spending time with his grandparents. Every Sunday, Joan, Benjamin, and Benji attended church together. Joan never forgot a special prayer for Patti.

Perhaps the most dramatic change was Gene's. Thumbing through the Sunday paper, Gene noticed an ad for a computer course, and somehow he accepted the possibility that the transition from tuning instruments to working computers was no big deal. Billy quickly got a gig playing backup for some bubblegummers. His approach was practical: music was music, whatever the beat.

Joe and Bu continued their routine back at Marsh Allan Products. Working close to one another helped pass the time. Uneventful days turned into uneventful weeks, and finally months. It was summer. When the whistle blew, the workers dashed from the plant, jumped into their cars, and squealed out of the lot. Joe and Bu climbed in Joe's Toyota pickup. They were both dirty from work and tired as usual. Bu lit up a joint.

"Where'd you get that?" Joe asked, his voice touched with enthusiasm. On the small amount of money they earned, grass was a luxury.

"Steve Dunn." Bu passed the joint to Joe. "Want some?"

Joe took a hit, and let his head fall back as he closed his eyes in anticipation of the calm of the high. "How much?" Joe passed the joint back.

"Only a buck. Steve said it's from Bolinas."

"Yeah." Joe laughed. "Bolinas, Ohio, most likely."

"Joe, what do you say to a quick stop at the Euc? Hear some, music, down a few brews?"

"Can't. Another time. I've gotta buy my mom a present. It's her birthday. What are you going to do?"

"Rehearse, probably."

"Rehearse? Rehearse what?" Joe looked bewildered.

"Oh, I didn't tell you 'cause it wasn't sure yet. I'm joining a new group—a Motown cover band." Bu joined in with Joe's laughter. "Seriously, it's damn good—seven-piece—mostly playing lounges now, but it could really break out. This white chick does terrific Smokey imitations."

"How's the money?"

"Real bad, but if I play 'Yesterday' one more time, my hand's gonna fall off. Forget about the brain damage!"

"What does Cindy think?"

"Well, she's trying to get pregnant, and that's not so easy. The extra money will help us, so I swallowed my pride—again. I ain't even trying to figure it out. We're playing the airport Holiday Inn. You oughta come. No buts or maybes."

Joe became pensive. "First, I gotta get a date. My mom's been bugging me about dating. She's even started fixing me up with chicks she meets at the beauty parlor! So I told her I already had a date. Now I gotta get one."

* * *

The birthday supper had seemed strange to Joe. The attempts not to mention Patti were strained, and there had been long periods of silence. Joe had also noticed that his mother seemed to have trouble keeping her concentration, and several times she had repeated earlier parts of the conversation. Joe was relieved when it came time to open his and Benji's gifts, a pair of bedroom slippers and a paperback book.

Ben went into the den to watch television while Joan and Joe carried the dishes into the kitchen. As Joan began to wash the dishes, Joe pulled a stool over to the sink for Benji to stand on. He could help them dry the dishes as they were passed along.

"I thought you were bringing a friend?" Joan sounded playful and mischievous, and also concerned.

"She couldn't make it." Joe shrugged.

"She's got a lot of nerve!"

"It's kind of nice, in a way, doing dishes by hand." Joe was relieved to be changing the subject. "Like old times. But what's wrong with the dishwasher?"

"Don't be stupid. We don't have a dishwasher."

"Huh?" Joe was alarmed now.

"But Gram, it's right there!" Benji laughed, pointing to the dishwasher. Maybe this was a game.

"What is, Benji?"

"The dishwasher!"

Joan paused and then looked to her right. The dishwasher was there, of course. Joan collected herself quickly. She made light of her mistake. "Oh! That old thing! Well, it makes noise. And it doesn't even work anymore."

Joe took a plate from Benji's hand and stacked it with the others. "Anyway, it's good for Benji. He probably never knew you could do dishes by hand, did you, Bongo Boy? So you learned something new. Now you can go and play." Joe lifted Benji from the stool and pointed him toward the living room. "Just keep your hands out of the fish tank!"

"Joe, I would think a young man like you would have all the girls after you."

"I've got girlfriends," he lied.

"Well, you can't get married without girlfriends. And Benji needs a mother. We don't know anything about the father, and Patti—"

"We don't discuss Patti!" Joe cut in. "Never!" Joan was taken aback by Joe's anger. Joe immediately regretted losing control. "Ma, sit down a second, I've got a surprise for you." Joe set his mother in a kitchen chair and opened a buffet drawer. He removed an envelope and handed it to her.

"But you already gave me a birthday present, Joe."

"This is a second one. It's your lucky day. It's

95

the final payment on your loan. I know it took awhile, but it's all there." Joan's eyes filled with tears.

"You're my pride and joy, Joe. I just thank God that he gave me two children." Joan stood up and gave Joe a warm hug. At that moment, Joe felt somehow more sad than happy. "Why don't you go in with your father. I'll wash the rest of the dishes."

"Sure." Joe walked into the den. His father was watching a baseball game, but he noticed Joe come into the room. Ben looked up, smiling, and made a gesture with his hand for Joe to sit on the couch next to him.

"Hi, son."

"How's the game?"

"You can turn it off. I wasn't watching."

"What's wrong with the dishwasher? Mom says it makes too much noise."

"It always makes too much noise."

"But it's *not* broken?"

Ben tried to dismiss Joe's obvious concern. "She gets confused." He turned to face Joe, and took his hand. "You know she really enjoys having you around to talk to. I never really know what to say." Ben took a pack of cigarettes out of his shirt pocket and lit one for Joe, too. His voice sounded wistful, and Joe felt drawn to his father. Joe shared his melancholy. "I wanted to talk to Patti, too.

You know, when she was having problems, but I didn't know what to say to her either. I guess I don't understand women much."

Joe was touched by his father's sincerity. "You just say what you feel."

"You make it sound easy." Benjamin laughed.

Joe sat forward. "Dad, I think Mother seems to be getting worse."

"She just gets confused. She has a bad day now and then, but nothing serious. A couple weeks ago she went around turning on all the lights."

"Has she seen a doctor?"

"Look. She's fine. Most of the time. Maybe there's nothing wrong."

"But shouldn't you discuss it with her?"

"Yeah, I suppose. I will. I just don't want to upset her. You know, we got a good life. We don't talk much or go out much, but I can't complain." Ben sat silent for a moment and looked down. The room seemed very still and quiet, even though Joe could hear a commercial on the television. Ben looked back up at Joe. "She gave me faith. What else is there?"

Joe kept his promise to Bu and went to see the Flashlights his new band. Joe even had a date; her name was Laurie. She was blond and twenty-two, and Joe thought she was very dignified. He had never asked her out before because she was Benji's play instructor at school. Joe had talked to her many times when he came to pick Benji up. She always acted friendly enough, and seemed genuinely fond of Benji. Joe wasn't sure that it was appropriate to ask her out, but that was before he had become really desperate. He didn't want to go to see Bu and his band alone, and he couldn't think of anyone else to ask on such short notice. And little Benji was with them, and this made Joe feel less awkward. it made the "date" more appropriate, somehow.

Laurie was wearing a dress, and at first Joe felt a bit self-conscious in his usual jeans and a "Cleveland Rocks" T-shirt. Maybe he should have dressed up. Laurie looked like a real teacher.

Joe and Laurie watched the Flashlights with real delight. The band was damn good. Good for what, Joe wasn't sure, but they did spirited versions of the best old Motown songs. A miniskirted blonde sang lead, and two thirty-ish black men backed her up. Bu seemed very happy to be playing bass again. Benji was jumping up and down, excited to see his "Uncle" Bu on stage.

The North Coast lounge in the Holiday Inn offered familiar, unthreatening decor: laminated wood tables, canvas chairs, potted trees, and a salad bar. Laurie was very impressed. Joe and Laurie exchanged furtive glances as the band performed the Miracles' hit, "I Second That Emotion." After several beers, Joe was feeling cool.

Laurie was still nursing her first mixed drink. They applauded when the band finished their set.

"She was just terrific!" Laurie gushed. "I loved it! If you closed your eyes, you'd think she was black!" Joe smiled as Laurie continued to rave. "Between classes and work, I never get out—particularly to places like this. It's like another world."

"It is," Joe said. "It's a Holiday Inn."

"You like it, Benji?" Laurie laughed. Benji raised his tiny fist like a rocker. Laurie checked her watch. "When does he have to be back?"

"Don't worry about Bongo." Bu and Roger, one of the black backups, approached the table. Joe waved them over.

"Uncle Bu, Uncle Bu!" yelled Benji.

"Give me five, Benji." They touched hands. "So what did ya think, Joe?"

"Real tight. A good set. Hi, Roger. Laurie, these are my friends Bu and Roger." Laurie smiled at them politely.

"Oh, I thought you guys were just great!" Bu and Roger pulled chairs up to the table and sat down.

"When was the last time I saw you, Joe?" Roger asked. "What group you with now?"

"Nobody. I'm just writing lyrics." Joe felt a brief sense of longing for the old days, the days he had been in the Barbusters with Bu and Patti. Joe let go of the thought.

"Hey, Bu. You guys get house drinks?" Bu laughed at Joe's crack. "Let's order another round."

As the group spoke more and more about music, Laurie felt lost. She busied herself playing with Benji. She looked a bit lost, as if she were out of her element and perhaps wished she hadn't come.

"I saw something about Patti in *Scene*," Roger broke in. "They're in Akron next week. How's she doing?" Benji perked up at the mention of Patti's name. Joe censored him with a glance.

"I don't know," Joe answered quietly.

"I hear she almost makes them good," Roger continued, with a big laugh.

"Who's Patti?" Laurie asked, suddenly curious.

"Benji's mother. My sister."

"Oh." Laurie was about to ask some polite questions about Patti, but Joe and his friends started to trade band talk, telling story after story about bands Laurie had never heard of before. No one seemed to pay any attention to her, and Benji had fallen asleep in his chair. Laurie felt distant from Joe and his friends. She started to wonder why she had come in the first place. She stood up, straightened her skirt, and interrupted the conversation. "Excuse me, I'll be right back," she said politely. "It was nice meeting you, Bu. And Roger." She then walked off.

Bu leaned over to Joe. "Nice girl. Do you think she's coming back?"

"Give me a little room, garbage mouth," Joe shot back. "I'm trying to improve myself."

"Sure you are." Bu looked across the room and yelled to a cocktail waitress, "Hey, turkey tits! A little service please." The guys started laughing, and Joe couldn't resist their good spirits. He laughed with them.

10 Joe knew the time was nearing when he would have to see Patti again. Benji had started asking about his mom more frequently, and Joe missed her. But it was obvious that Patti wasn't going to be the one to make the first move. Joe needed to say something to Benji, and he waited until one night when they were in the bathtub together. Joe was washing Benji's back as Benji played with the bathwater.

"Benji, do you remember last week, you asked me about Mom?"

Benji stood up in the tub and faced Joe. "That was last week!" He splashed water in Joe's face.

"This is important."

"I'm all done with my bath, Dad."

"Don't call me that!" Joe said firmly. "Call me Joe or Uncle Joe."

"I'm cold, Uncle Joe," Benji said quite naturally, not really thinking about the significance of Joe's remark. Joe gave him a hug, and helped him out of the tub. He dried Benji off and put him in his terry-cloth robe. After Joe put his own robe on, he took Benji by the hand into the living room. He handed Benji his plastic guitar.

"Let me see your stance," Joe said. Benji's face showed real joy now. Guitar practice with Uncle Joe was one of his favorite times. Benji assumed the posture of a rock-and-roller. Joe couldn't help smiling at Benji's delight. "You listen to me. I'm gonna teach you something. Anything you can say, you can sing. That's all lyrics are. People talking. Now let's try an experiment. I'll just turn on the television, and the first words we hear, we'll sing."

The television came on, and the screen filled with a picture of a man in close-up, declaiming, "You got no place to go." Joe shut the TV off, and sat with Benji on the couch. Joe picked up his own guitar.

"Now what's good for you Key of C?" he asked Benji, one rock-and-roller to another.

"Yeah." Benji giggled.

Joe started strumming his guitar, and Benji imitated him. Then Joe began singing, over and over, "You got no place to go." Benji joined in, and they kept repeating the phrase over and over until they were caught up in a fit of laughter. Joe put his guitar down and picked Benji up. He sat with Benji in his lap, holding him close. Thoughts of Patti came to him. The room seemed to be haunted by her presence. Joe had seen ads for the Hunzz in the paper. They were playing the Akron Agora, a converted playhouse that was having a Monster Metalmania weekend. Joe knew that, finally, he would go and talk to his sister.

The Akron Agora marquee screamed in bright, clashing neons: APPEARING TONIGHT: GATES OF PURGATORY, THE HUNZZ, THE B-BALLS. As a sweaty mass of fans came stumbling out the exit doors, Joe elbowed his way inside. He pushed past the crowd of young males, aimless and angry in torn, heavy-metal T-shirts and uniforms of denim and leather. These kids were branded unemployable.

A Twisted Sister video blared from monitors above the bar. It was less music than physical assault: ninety-five percent vibration, five percent melody. Joe asked the bartender where the dressing rooms were, then followed his directions down the hall into a cavernous room, its walls covered with slogans and sketches, a hieroglyphic history of one-night stands and defunct bands. Two members of the Gates of Purgatory rested on a Goodwill sofa, and a couple of B-Balls, still dressed in their red rubber costumes, posed by a lone video game against the wall.

Patti sat at a small table, removing the last of her makeup and smoking a cigarette at the same time. She recognized Joe first.

"Hey, little brother," she called.

"Patti?" Joe answered, stunned for a second. This creature looked more like Vampira than his sister. Her face was hard, and her black dress looked trashy and used.

"Sit down." Patti pointed to a chair with her cigarette.

"Did you see the show?"

"No." He didn't intend to hide the fact that he'd intentionally missed it, but Patti rambled on without noticing.

"Too bad. We were hot! Did you see the B-Balls? The kids in the rubber suits?"

"No, I saw them. I didn't hear them."

"They used to open for us. Then they got those suits." Patti laughed. "Now we open for them!"

Billy Tettore walked in, his Hunzz makeup half scrubbed off, and did a double take when he saw Patti and Joe together. "Hey! Ozzie and Harriet! How are you?"

Joe smiled and shook Billy's hand, wondering if perhaps the kid was wearing a fright wig. "It's going all right," he managed to say before asking, "What's going on with your hair? I didn't know you were a Hun."

"Oh, just filling in for a week," Billy replied self-consciously.

"Yeah." Patti laughed. "We have a lot of turnover. I'm one of the three 'original' Hunzz now."

"Hey, Joe. Look at this." Billy showed Joe his forearms. Each was boldly tattooed with a sequence of numbers: 371-46-4118. "What do you think?"

"Great," Joe said, a little revolted.

"Isn't it neat? It's my Social Security number."

Joe looked away and laughed. "That's good thinking."

"I had it done when I was with another band." Billy chuckled.

Joe and Patti remained silent.

"Look, I gotta split and I'm sure you both got a lot of things to talk about. Nice seeing you."

"Nice seeing you, too." Joe waved. "Be careful with that mousse."

Joe and Patti sat in glum silence for a full minute after Billy left. Finally, Joe had to break the silence, the tension. He pulled some folded papers from his pocket and handed them to Patti.

"Listen, I brought you something, some lyrics I wrote. Just some ideas. I thought you might want to use them." Joe felt more and more awkward as he spoke. "You don't have to use them." Patti took the lyrics, hesitated, then tucked them away.

"Is this why you came?" She let her cigarette

fall to the floor as Joe shook his head. "Why?" she challenged.

"I knew you were here. Look, Benji starts school in the fall, and he's all excited. I've got a picture here if you want—"

"Look!" Patti broke in. "Benji don't belong to me right now. He belongs to Mother. You know it can only be one way or the other."

"Yeah, but I can arrange for you to see Bongo without Mom knowing. I could set it up." Joe tried to conceal his frustration. "I mean, goddammit, it just gets hard to explain." Joe was sure he was being totally reasonable.

"Okay." Patti's voice was vague and without feeling.

"When?" Joe was becoming more anxious.

"Soon," she answered evasively. "I'll get in touch." She stood up and started pacing back and forth.

"Why are you doing all this? What are you trying to prove?" Joe stood too, unable to control his impatience and anger.

"Nothing, exactly nothing. You're the one who's trying to prove something."

"Bullshit—I got nothing to prove."

"You paid Mom back the six hundred bucks for the tools, right?" Patti was standing in front of Joe now, glaring.

"Who told you?" he answered defensively.

"Nobody. Nobody had to. I know you're dumb

enough to pay her back. For what?" Patti's voice started to rise in anger. "Thought you could be free? Instead, you accept her values—"

"What the fuck is this?" Joe exploded. "Since when did Mom invent the system where you pay back all your debts? This is crazy, you're all twisted sideways. I'm just trying to live by some common"—Joe paused, searching for the word—"sense."

Patti took Joe's hands in hers. "That's why you don't understand me! We were real close, but you never had the slightest idea what I was up to. You see those idiots over there?" Patti nodded toward some other musicians, slouching in the distance. "They think they're gonna be stars! They want to do deals and demos and limos." Patti became accusatory, making it sound like making it big was wrong or silly. "You ever heard me talk like that, Joe? No, you didn't, 'cause I go out there every night just to hear the beat." Patti pounded the table with her fists and started making strange guitar sounds, one assault after another. Suddenly, she stopped and seemed to calm down. "That's all there is, man."

Joe didn't comprehend. He didn't understand the connection between all this and his idea that Patti see Benji. "Is that what I'm supposed to tell Benji when I put him to bed? Maybe you should just tape this little speech so I can play it for him?"

"Benji can figure it out for himself." Patti paused,

and then said, with bitterness, "After all, he's got two good teachers."

Defeated, Joe said, "You know what I think?"

Patti exploded, "I don't care what you think! You don't understand anything. You're ignorant!"

Joe was about to explode himself, but he pulled back. He was going to remain calm. "Look, I'm sorry this happened. I didn't come here to fight. Say good-bye to Billy for me." Joe walked quickly out the door, not even wanting to hear what Patti might have left to say.

11 Weeks passed and neither Joe nor Patti attempted to speak to one another. Joe had simply willed himself back into the drudgery of work at Marsh Allan Products, Inc. Little did he realize his routine was about to be interrupted.

Joe and Bu were eating lunch in a quiet storage room in the factory. They sat on top of unpacked storage crates, thermoses, and waxed paper spread around them. Bright sunlight streamed through dirty glass windows, overlooking the gray, vaguely depressing Cleveland skyline. But the dreariness didn't bother the men as they laughed and relaxed.

". . . and now he says he's gonna buy a VCR for his van," Bu was saying. "He's got so much stuff he buys magazines to figure out more stuff to buy. Stuff that he can't use and . . ." He stopped speaking as he noticed Joe looking at him very strangely. "What?" he asked.

"Did you lose weight?" Joe asked simply.

"No." Bu smiled. "I shaved my beard off."

"Then how come Cindy still has that rash?" Joe snickered.

Suddenly the foreman came rushing up to them, calling, "Joe, I've been looking for you in the lunchroom." Joe immediately wondered what he'd done wrong.

"Yeah, well," replied Bu, "we like to eat near the tubing."

The foreman approached, out of breath. "You got a call. Your mother's in the hospital. They want you there."

Joe practically flew to his truck and sped off toward Booth Hospital. Damn! What had happened? His mind was reeling—I hope it's not too late. I told Dad to take her to a doctor—he blared his horn and swerved to pass the crawling traffic, his knuckles white.

As soon as Joe stepped from the elevator in the hospital, he saw his father standing and staring into space. He was wearing his work suit, a J. C. Penny standard, a striped tie, and a name tag.

"What happened?" Joe asked breathlessly, fearing the answer.

"I finally got her to see Dr. Natterson. She'd been feeling really tired, and getting more confused. Natterson decided to put her in here for tests."

"But how is she?" Joe pressed on.

"I don't know." The weariness and confusion showed on Ben's face. "They just keep going in and out, taking tests, and talking about more tests."

"What do they say?"

"Nothing. Yet. She's resting. They got her a room."

"Where's Benji?"

"At our friend's the Shepleys. He thinks it's a sleep-over. Come say hello to your mother. She'll be glad you're here."

Joan Rasnick sat stiffly in her hospital bed, watching daytime TV. A potted plant stood on the bed table and a crucifix hung on the wall above the headboard. Joe noticed that Joan's room had a dingy view of railroad tracks. He walked cautiously to her and kissed her. She took his hand.

"Hi, Mom."

"Don't you look good." Joan seemed unworried. She beamed at her son and patted his hand.

"What are you watching?" Joe asked.

"I'm watching 'Another World.'" Joan's face turned serious. "You want to know something crazy? They have all different characters on it here!" Joe and his father shot each other a concerned look. "I don't recognize any of these. What do you suppose they did to the other ones?"

Joe had to change the topic. "How do you feel?"

"I feel the way you'd feel if you'd been poked everyhere there is to be poked all day. I told these doctors I have to get home for dinner. I said my son was coming over." Joan spoke with love and pride for Joe.

"You're going to be all right."

"I just want it to be over." Joan stopped to think and then looked back up at Ben and Joe. "I'd be perfectly all right if I didn't snack so much. Snacking. That's all it is." Again, Joan became silent.

"Ma?" Joe said to her, as if to get back her attention.

"Oh, I'm so sorry. I was waiting for you to come, but now I feel so tired. I think I just need a little nap."

"Sure, Ma. You go to sleep. I'll come by again tomorrow."

That night, Joe went alone to the Rascal House. He heard the pings and pongs of video games before he entered the arcade. Joe remembered that Patti occasionally came here to relax and forget. Maybe it could work for him, too.

At home, Benjamin Rasnick sat alone, wornout, sipping a cup of coffee at the kitchen table. Dear God, he thought, take care of my wife. Let her be well. Don't let her suffer. Whatever happens, please don't let her suffer.

* * *

The next day, Joe, in slacks and a white shirt, sat with his father in the hospital waiting area. Reverend Ansley was with them. He was an old family friend who was about forty-five years old. He wore a dark navy suit, and his manner was both intelligent and direct. Two doctors, Dr. Natterson, in street clothes, and Dr. Gould, in a white jacket, walked toward them. After greeting one another, Dr. Natterson and Reverend Ansley locked arms: these men were old comrades in bedside combat.

"Hello Joe," said Dr. Natterson. "This is Dr. Gould. He's an oncologist."

"What's that?" Joe asked. He was sure he had never heard the word before.

"A cancer specialist," Gould replied. "The biopsy on your mother was positive. We want to do an exploratory operation the day after tomorrow." Joe was stunned. He stepped back involuntarily. Those two words—cancer and operation—shook his entire body and mind with a power he had never known words could have. He looked at his father. Benjamin's expression indicated that he already knew his wife's condition.

"If the malignancy is localized," Dr. Gould kept talking, "we'll cut it out right then."

"What's the rush?" asked Joe, still bewildered. "We've hardly had time to fill out the hospital papers yet."

"Let me explain." Dr. Natterson was talking

now, his hand on Joe's shoulder. He was trying to be as sympathetic as possible. "Your mother has ovarian cancer. In itself, that's not so serious, since the ovaries can be cut out." Cut. Out. Again, these words frightened Joe. "But in a woman her age there are no symptoms, no discharge, until the cancer moves somewhere else. We have to find out how far it's spread."

Joe looked at his father, but Ben looked away. Meeting Joe's glance at that moment would be too painful.

That night, after Joe had a quiet dinner with his father, he didn't go home. Instead, he drove by the hospital and parked his car across the street. He peered through the windshield, across the street to the windows of his mother's room. He put on the car radio. Bob Seger was singing something slow, a sad and wistful song, with his plaintive voice. What was becoming of their family, wondered Joe; Patti lost to heavy metal, and his mother losing to cancer. And Benji. Poor Benji. He thought his grandma had just gone to visit someone for a few days. Soon he would have to know the truth.

Joe went to the hospital alone the next day. He walked into his mother's room and found Reverend Ansley and Ben sitting at her bedside. An open bible rested on her lap. Joan smiled, and Joe was suddenly struck by the thought that the doctors had spent the day carving lines on her face. He leaned across the bed to kiss her.

"Hello, Mom. Dad. Reverend."

"Hello, Joe," said Reverend Ansley a kind smile on his face.

"How's Benji?" asked Joan.

"He's staying with Bu and Cindy. I'll bring him by tonight. How do you feel, Ma?"

"I'm getting a little tired with all this lying around." Joan laughed. "And I've got so much work to do at home." Joe smiled. An awkward silence fell. The only sounds were footsteps in the corridor—the brisk walk of nurses and the slow shuffle of patients.

"Sid Natterson is a good Christian man, Joe. And he's also a good physician." Joan was mentioning the things she knew Joe dared not bring up. "God will guide his hand during the operation."

"Yes," Joe whispered.

"Is Patti here?"

"No," Joe answered, feeling lost. "I haven't had time to reach her."

"Well, that's all right. I understand if she can't make it. I know she's got a lot to do." Joan's voice was sympathetic, not at all resentful, Joe could only swallow hard. Just then, the sound of an approaching train began filling the room, the clatter of its wheels carried by the wind into the open window, the haunting whistle blowing.

"I wonder if we could all join in prayer?" asked Reverend Ansley, now standing. They linked hands and started in the words of the Lord's Prayer. The screaming of the train was louder now, as if trying to combat the prayer. The wheels roared against the tracks, the engine blasted, and the scream of the whistle became urgent and shrill. It's music, thought Joe as he mouthed the prayer. Heavy-metal music.

12 The speakers at the 555 Club, tucked in the fiery shadows of a Pittsburgh steel mill, blasted so loud it was like a fist in the face; the volume neared the pain threshold. Joe looked at the crowd: young, angry, drunk, aching for violence. Only the jackhammer beat of the music subdued them—music loud enough to blow the mills from their minds. Joe kept pushing through the hostile crowd. Ahead, obscured in smoke, the Hunzz were playing in red crosslight.

Patti stalked the stage. She was in full metal drag, her face afire, all flames and flares. Sweat smeared her makeup. Her gravel voice belted out a repetitive, abrasive refrain. Silhouetted by a floor-level white spot, Patti was a vision of hellish intensity. Obscene shouts from the crowd punctuated her vocals. Patti played with the mike stand, treating it like a sex object. Joe stood at the end of the bar. This was his sister. He had never seen her so possessed.

Joe's pickup sped through the Ohio night. Patti was slumped in the shotgun seat, legs propped on the dashboard, face scrubbed clean. They rambled through darkness drinking beers in silence.

It was dawn when they finally arrived at the hospital. They plodded their way past the admitting desk. Patti's belt chains rattled against her studs. Joe was unshaven. Neither bothered to notice the stares they attracted.

Outside Joan's room, Joe and Patti greeted their father and Reverend Ansley. Patti and her father, never really sure of what to do, just shook hands. Reverend Ansley gave Patti's wardrobe a once-over, his disapproval masked by a sympathetic smile.

"Patti, I'm so glad you could come," Reverend Ansley said with a small smile forming at the corners of his mouth. Patti immediately stepped back defensively. She had obviously never liked or respected this man.

"Can we go in?" asked Joe.

"She's already in pre-op," answered the reverend. "She won't be out until late this afternoon."

Ben looked at his children through bloodshot eyes. "Why don't you rest?" he suggested.

Joe put a protective arm around Patti as they walked slowly away, wishing they could see their mother, only slightly relieved to leave the hospital's aura of death behind.

The Toyota pulled into Patti and Joe's driveway. This was a reassuring tableau; on the surface nothing had changed. Patti and Joe had not slept in over thirty hours. Exhausted, they got out of the pickup and pulled themselves into the house.

Cindy had stayed to watch Benji, and both their faces lit up at the sight of Patti. Benji ran across the room to Patti's open arms. Patti was trembling, but on seeing Benji she felt a surge of energy overtake her. She wrapped her arms around him, clasping him to her breast. She hid her face in his, kissing him again and again.

"Mommy, Mommy, Mommy," Benji repeated over and over as he held his mother close to him.

"Benji. I've missed you so much," Patti said, her voice breaking with emotion. She fought to regain her composure.

"I missed you, Patti," said Cindy, but Patti was too involved with Benji to hear her.

"C'mon, Benji, let's go to your room. Let's read something together." She could hardly believe her child was in her arms again. She wanted to say it seemed like they'd never been apart, but she knew

121

that was a lie. Simply seeing Benji made her realize how much must have changed in his life since she'd left. And her life . . . She fought back the tears and smiled at her beautiful boy. "Did you get new school clothes?" Benji nodded happily. "Show me," she whispered, and she carried him upstairs, feeling more like a mother than she had in years.

As soon as Cindy was out the door, Joe collapsed on the sofa.

At the hospital the next day, Joe sat with his father in Dr. Natterson's nondescript office. Dr. Gould, the cancer specialist, was with them.

"Unfortunately, the cancer has spread into the liver, the intestines, and the pancreas. If we had tried to remove all of it, we would have lost her on the table. So we sewed her up."

Ben Rasnick grimaced and turned his head away from the doctors.

"What's next?" asked Joe, his voice very troubled.

"Chemotherapy, but that's only if you make that decision."

"Joe, where's Patti?" asked Benjamin, as though not hearing the mention of chemotherapy.

"She went right to Ma's room."

Patti was wearing a plaid flannel shirt and jeans. She wore little makeup and carried a package with her. She took a deep breath before opening the door to her mother's room. Get-well cards and floral bouquets filled the available shelf space. Joan was in bed resting. Patti was taken aback when she saw her mother's face. The operation had taken a toll. Joan's face was gaunt, and she seemed very tired.

Patti walked over to her mother's bed, bent down, and kissed her on the cheek. "Mom, I'm so sorry," Patti half whispered.

"Patti, I'm so glad you came. I knew you'd come when you found a chance. Did you see Benji? Doesn't he look good? And your music. I want to hear about that, too." Not quite knowing what to say, Joan kept trying to say it all.

"Slow down, Ma. We'll be spending lots of time together. We'll talk about lots of stuff. Are they taking good care of you?"

"Oh, the best. They all seem like very nice, thoughtful people. I have their expertise, and I have their prayers."

"I brought you something, Mom," said Patti, opening the package.

"What is it?"

"It's a Simon game," Patti said, removing a large saucer-shaped plastic toy. Different-colored squares formed a circle around the game. "You play it like Simple Simon. It used to be popular a long time ago. It took me all morning to find one." Patti placed the game on her mother's lap. "Watch: I press blue, and then the machine repeats. I press blue and any other color, like red, and the machine repeats again. Then you repeat. If you get a sequence wrong, the machine buzzes and you lose."

They started to play the game together. Joan's eyes twinkled like a child's as she pressed the colored squares. After a couple of moves, the machine buzzed. "Shoot!" exclaimed Joan. "Let's play again." Joan pressed several of the squares and then paused. "Oh, I can't remember if I pressed red-yellow or yellow-red." They laughed. "Tell you what," said Joan, "I'll practice by myself, then we'll play again in a few days." Patti got up and took the game and placed it on one of the end tables.

"Are you and Joe getting along?" Joan asked.

"No problem."

"I told him how much I was looking forward to seeing you. He's such a good boy, like his father. It's hard not to get along with Joe." Joan turned to Patti. "You know, I almost married somebody else. His name was John Palsrock. Oh, he was a card. Always cutting up, telling jokes. Honestly, we laughed until we were sick sometimes. But he wasn't a responsible person. Then I met your father and married him.

"You know, when I think about all these decicions—and I think about them a lot—I think that all the big ones, the small ones, they all seem the same to me. I mean, you marry Ben Rasnick, not John Palsrock, you press red, not yellow. I decide to marry, or I decide not to marry. I decide to have a child, or I decide not to have a child. It's all the same."

Joan reached out and took Patti's hand. She felt confused, but she struggled to understand. Somehow, she thought, Patti and I just don't think alike. She wondered why. Joan had been able to understand and accept her own parent's values. What had gone wrong? What had she failed to do or say that Patti had drifted so much? I'll have to think more about that, Joan told herself. But she was very tired from the drugs. Despite her efforts to stay awake, she gradually drifted off to sleep.

13 On Friday night, Joe and Patti had to get out of the house to escape the pressure. They decided to meet Bu, Cindy, and Gene at the Euclid Tavern, the site where the Barbusters once had a local following and a good reputation. The others agreed to get there early and start getting loaded while Patti waited for Benji's baby-sitter.

By the time Patti joined them the Euc was beginning to get crowded. On stage, three college kids were setting up their synthesizers. They were the "newest" local bar band in Cleveland. By midnight, the bar was packed five deep with teens in search of each other and a good time. The group had just ordered another pitcher of beer when Gene saw Patti walking toward them. She was wearing her Hunzz black outfit, minus the chains and the studs.

"Hey Patti!" Gene called out to her. Patti pulled a chair up to the table. She sat down and lit a cigarette, then filled a glass of beer and quickly downed it.

"Sorry to hear about your mom," said Bu. "It's a real kick in the ass."

"I know," Patti told him. "We just had to get out of the house."

"How's your dad?" Cindy asked with concern.

"Asleep. He's full of Valium. They got him a nurse." Patti took another drag on her cigarette.

"What are you gonna do now?" asked Gene.

"Hang around, I guess. The Hunz already broke up." Just then, Joe noticed two girls passing by. He got up from the table in hot pursuit of the one with bigger breasts.

"Oogie offered the old Barbusters a gig here in two weeks."

For the first time in ages, Patti let a big grin form on her face. "I know. I took it. How about it?"

"Shit yes," said Bu. "I love the Euc."

"The Puke!" joked Gene, raising his beer glass in a toast. Across the room Patti could see Joe saying something to the two girls that sent them both fleeing. Patti let out a laugh.

"Who are they?" Patti asked, pointing to the band on stage.

"One of Oog's cut-rate specials," Bu said. "They used to be called Sins. Now they're just Problems!"

"Let's get drunk," suggested Patti, raising her glass. The group cheered and downed their beer. The Problems were playing a Talking Heads–like version of "True Love Ways." Was Patti already that drunk, or did the group sound something like a band from a Polynesian Village hotel lounge? They certainly sounded strange.

As the hours wore on, the bar started to empty. A determined wife strong-armed her protesting husband out the door, while a white-faced student staggered toward the john. They felt no pain. Joe, more tipsy now, approached a well-dressed girl walking across the room. He stood in front of her, temporarily blocking her passage.

"What's the difference between a scumbag and the Eiffel Tower?" Joe asked the girl, more drunkenly than good-natured.

"The Eiffel Tower doesn't come on to girls like me!" The girl sneered at Joe; walking right past him.

The Problems had finished their set, and the stage was bare except for their equipment. Bu was sitting on the stage, next to a synthesizer. With a good-natured grin, he watched Joe's futile attempts to score for the evening. Poor Joe, thought Bu, no matter how he approaches a chick, he still comes on like a kid. Maybe he projected too much sincerity. Joe walked over to Bu and sat down next to him. He lit a cigarette.

"You know, Bu," slurred Joe, "the Barbusters were a great band."

"We were good," agreed Bu, his voice expressing all his longing for what were now the good old days. "Joe," Bu continued, "I want to tell you something I've never told anybody else before."

"Yeah, buddy, what's that?" said Joe, bracing himself.

"I always had the hots for Patti!" Bu laughed nervously.

Joe felt his whole body and face turn warm and tense. Bu. Even Bu. Every damn body had the hots for Patti! Everybody but Joe. He couldn't. They were brother and sister. He wasn't sure why, but Joe felt uneasy thinking about Patti and other guys. He had never imagined Patti with Bu.

"No big deal." Joe smiled as he tried to sound matter-of-fact.

"I always figured sometime, somewhere on the road, we'd make it." He paused and reflected for a moment. "But it never happened," he concluded. Bu was talking to himself as much as to Joe, who was watching Patti slow-dance in front of the stage with Gene. Joe glowered as he saw Gene, enamored, holding Patti's waist as they moved together.

Gene spoke softly to Patti. "And all the time I thought you thought I was just a dumb jock.

130

After all, I'm just a roadie. You all were the musicians, the important ones."

Patti stroked the back of Gene's neck. "No. You were the backbone of the band. You were the most important person."

"Really?" Gene asked, surprised. He couldn't tell if Patti was putting him on or being sincere. But it was nice of her to say, anyway. They danced past Joe, who looked like he was sulking.

The night didn't end. Somehow Cindy, Bu, Gene, Patti, and Joe were still walking, talking, and dancing. The sorrow of Joan's illness and the nostalgia of the band being together again created a melancholy mood. They had all been drinking too much, but none of them got drunk. It was as though Patti and Joe had to find their way to a special moment alone. They had spoken around each other all night; now they had to speak *to* each other, to fulfill the deep need to be close once more. They were now on the dance floor together, rocking back and forth, belly to belly, crotch to crotch, more like lovers than siblings.

"You know, I always had this dream," Patti was telling Joe as they continued to hold each other close. Her speech was slow, her voice hoarse from that night's accumulation of beer and cigarettes and nonstop talking. "We were on stage together, surrounded by friends we could see who couldn't see us. And the only sound was music."

"When did this dream end?" asked Joe.

"Never."

"It's not my dream," Joe said evenly.

"What is?"

"I don't know. It's got music in it. And a girl, somewhere. You're no help. Every girl I wanted I compared to you—and that ended that." Joe sounded very alone and lost. "How come we never talked about this before? It's not like we didn't have a chance to talk."

"I don't know, Joe. I just don't know." Patti held Joe closer. He was right. They had never talked about real things, about feelings and longings. They always seemed to be working on music or arguing about their mother. But this was so much better. Patti felt an emotional bond with Joe, and she hoped it could last.

The following week, Joe and Patti did their best to continue life "as usual." The fact that their mother was growing worse made them more sensitive to one another. They tried to avoid any topics that would erupt into destructive quarrels. They were, in more than a manner of speaking, on their best behavior.

Patti cleaned the house. She even attempted to put their record collection into some semblance of order. At first, she thought about arranging groups by type of music. But that wasn't so simple. Rock had splintered into so many subsections—country rock, pop, dance, rap, retro rock—that she finally decided plain old alphabetical order would have to do. Patti made make sure to take Benji to school each day and then pick him up at the end of the afternoon. Sometimes she even went to play group and mixed in with the other mothers and children.

Joe and Bu continued to stamp trays at Marsh Allan Products, Inc. Time had passed, and in an effort to keep up with current fashion, the "Charles and Di" trays were now "Andrew and Fergie" trays. Joe couldn't believe there were so many of them. Sometimes he wondered if these trays reproduced themselves at night when no one was looking. In the evening, when Joe got home, he would sit on the sofa with Benji and play guitar. Benji had a new "professional model," a K-Mart five-string. They continued to work on the song they had started a couple weeks earlier, adding a new verse each night.

One night, Patti, Cindy, Bu, and Joe went to the Symposium, a country bar in west Cleveland. A faded U.S. flag hung behind the stage. The adjoining walls flowed with a variety of beer signs. Billy had taken still another replacement gig as a drummer in a country band, the Old Boys, a "Waylon-n-Willie" cover band. Joe and Patti shared a laugh over Billy's versatility. As long as a band, any band, anywhere, needed a drummer, Billy would be available.

Perhaps Ben Rasnick had the most difficult time.

He wasn't used to being on his own. He made frozen dinners, most of which went half eaten. As he watched television, he looked through old family albums. He allowed himself to cry. But the toughest part was going to sleep, because he simply couldn't adjust to his bed without Joan. Its emptiness was the most painful reminder of her illness. Ben would kneel in prayer before wrestling with sleep. In bed, he read a variety of religious pamphlets on hope and courage and God's will. Thank God, Ben thought, thank God I have belief. Joan had taught him the power of prayer and the solace of belief. He thanked God for Joan.

14 Two nurses were trying to draw blood from Joan Rasnick's arm. Patti was sitting beside her mother, holding her other arm. Joe stood against the wall watching, his face pained over his helplessness to comfort his mother.

The older nurse was instructing the trainee about the correct procedure for removing blood. The trainee was nervous and unsure. She had stuck the needle in an impoverished vein, again, and couldn't seem to extract anything. Joan looked very tired and very ill. This was the first time Joe and Patti had seen her unkempt. Her hair was knotted and messy and wet with perspiration, and her face now truly showed the ordeal she had been undergoing. There seemed to be little strength left in her body. It was difficult to believe that Joan had only been in the hospital for three weeks.

"Oh!" said the younger nurse, upset at her failed attempt to find a "good" vein.

"Try another vein!" commanded the older nurse in a stern, strictly professional voice. "Just be a good girl," she ordered Mrs. Rasnick.

Joan grimaced in pain. "I don't want to be a good girl," she snapped at the nurse. There was still fire in her spirit. Joe looked away. He could hardly bear it.

"Can't you find someone a little more experienced?" Joe pleaded with the older nurse.

"Quiet, please. This is difficult." The nurse was getting more and more impatient. All Joe could do was watch as the trainee tried another vein.

Patti moved her mouth an inch from her mother's ear; her arm supporting her shoulders. Joan quivered spasmodically. Patti spoke into her mother's ear. Her voice sounded detached and soothing. "We are alone," Patti said. "Here, there is only the touch of my hand, the sound of my voice, the touch of my lips. Nothing else exists."

Joe was drawn closer to the bed by the soothing calm of Patti's voice. His eyes became moist with tears as he saw her drawing out their mother's pain. He had never seen Patti like this.

"Patti!" Joan cried, straining to be one with Patti.

"Mother," Patti whispered, her voice still calm. She was now crying. She drew her face even closer, until her head was resting on the pillow. "Mother, don't let them into our world. There's nothing else, no pain. We're isolated. Only you and I are in this room."

Joe turned away, so moved he couldn't stay in the room for another moment. He walked out the door and started down the corridor to where his father and Reverend Ansley were sitting in prefab chairs. Joe composed himself as they stood up. He smiled grimly and touched his father's sleeve.

"I always thought I'd go first," Ben Rasnick said flatly.

"Joe," Ansley said. "Can we talk for a minute?"

"Sure," replied Joe. "What's this all about?" Ansley led him down the hall. They stopped beside the hospital elevator.

"I want to talk about Patti," Ansley said, looking and sounding somber.

"What now?," asked Joe, a little put off.

"Watch out for her," Ansley stated sternly.

"Huh?" Joe was caught off guard.

"You've known me a long time. Not well, but long. I'm a reasonable man. I'm tolerant. I live in the real world. Your father and I have talked about this." Ansley frowned. Joe knew he was getting ready to deliver the kill. "Patti is dangerous."

Joe felt the blood rise to his head. He wanted to punch Ansley but knew he couldn't. He controlled his impulse, for his mother's sake. "Excuse my language, Reverened, but what is this shit?" Joe's voice rose in anger.

Ansley kept talking, like a man who knew he was being completely sensible. "Your sister believes in nothing. She doesn't care about family, church, or society. She doesn't care if the garbage gets collected or—"

"She helps Mother!" Joe interrupted. "That's all that matters now."

"Her brain is poisoned and now she's trying to poison her mother's," Ansley went on. "She's in there right now trying to strip Joan of one of the things she needs most—her faith. Every night I sit with your mother, fighting Patti's influence. Your mother's mind is weak. Patti's chosen this moment to get her revenge."

"I'm not gonna listen to this anymore," said Joe, and instead of waiting for the elevator, he turned and walked down the stairway.

Joe parked the Toyota in front of the house and turned it off. He sat unmoving, watching the house. A light went on, and he could see Patti wearing panties and a skimpy halter. She was playing with Benji, lifting him up and kissing him. It was good seeing Patti like this, so unlike the woman Reverend Ansley had described. There *was* good in Patti. Joe could see it. He kept watching, lost in thought. He remembered Ansley's words, and kept telling himself they just couldn't be true.

On Friday, Ben, Joe, Patti, and Benji all went to the hospital together. Each was more dressed up than usual: Ben and Joe wore jackets and slacks, Patti (for once) wore a dress, and Benji was in his Sunday best, a blue jacket with gray pants. They sat on a row of multicolored chairs outside Joan's room in the hospital corridor. Benji held Patti's hand as they made small talk about the weather and the hospital. No one mentioned Joan. Doctors Natterson and Gould stepped out of Joan's room. Natterson approached Patti.

"Your mother would like to see you alone," he said matter-of-factly. Patti and Joe stood simultaneously.

"Stay with Grandpa and Uncle Joe," Patti said to Benji. Patti entered her mother's room as Joe turned to Dr. Gould.

"Some job you got," Joe said to Dr. Gould in an attempt to show some feeling for him. "You must have to see patients like my mom every day."

"It's not so bad," said Dr. Gould. "Sometimes,

in a freak case like this, you can only stand and watch. Other times you can help and cure."

"Then why keep testing her?" Joe asked, expressing the frustration they all shared. "She doesn't need any more tests; she needs painkillers. Give her something."

"We just did." Dr. Gould glanced from Benjamin to Joe. "There won't be any more tests."

Joan steadied herself as Patti took a seat next to her bed. The game Patti had given her rested on the bed table. Joan's condition was markedly worse. Her poise and makeup couldn't disguise the aura of death.

"Could I be alone with my daughter please?" Joan asked the nurse. The nurse didn't budge.

"It's all right, ask Dr. Natterson," Patti told the nurse.

"I'll be right outside if you need me," said the nurse, unsmiling as she walked out of the room and closed the door behind her.

"I wanted to be alone with you," Joan told Patti. Patti remained silent. Joan wasn't sure of how she should begin. Avoiding what she really wanted to talk about, Joan glanced in the direction of the toy. "The Simon broke. I think I played it too much." She laughed.

"Maybe it needs new batteries."

"Dad got me new batteries. It still doesn't work."

"We'll get another."

"Is there anybody else waiting to see me?" Joan asked.

"No."

"It's so tiring to be friendly. Nobody likes to visit somebody who's depressed."

"You don't have to put on a show for us, Mom," Patti said, taking her mother's hand.

"They gave me a shot for pain, but it makes me dizzy. Sometimes I even talk crazy. If I talk crazy, just tell me. I'll stop."

"It's all right. You can talk any way you want to."

"There's nobody out there?" Joan asked again.

"No," Patti repeated. Patti poured her mother a glass of water. Patti could sense that something more was coming. They had avoided any substantive issues on areas of possible conflict, but they both knew there wasn't much time left. If important things were to be said, they would have to be said now. If emotional connections were to be made—if Patti and Joan were to really touch each other's lives—now was the time. Patti felt uneasy. This conversation had been postponed for a lifetime.

"I'm so tired, Patti. This has been such a painful time, but I don't want you to be sad."

"I know."

"This is not a sad time," Joan said with deep

conviction. She placed her glass of water back on the small table next to her bed.

"I'm not sad," Patti lied. She was hit by a surge of sorrow that her mother would not be with her much longer. She was sad that it would take her mother's death to resolve all that had gone before. Patti never anticipated that she could miss her mother, but here, in this hospital room, she was starting to miss her already. But what was Joan about to ask of her, Patti wondered. Would it be too much? Patti eyed her mother cautiously.

"I'm going to see my dad. I've missed him so much over the years." Joan's voice revealed a genuine sense of longing, as if she truly looked forward to the inevitable end of her life. "I'm looking forward to it. And I'll see my mother and baby brother too—Thomas. I've thought about him so often. I don't remember him. I was only three when he died. I've always wondered what he was like. Well, now I'm going to see him." Joan paused and glanced away from Patti to the open window. "I'm going to see them all."

"I'm happy for you." Patti was amazed that her mother seemed so truly unafraid.

"Is Joe dating?" Joan asked, now looking right at Patti. The sudden change of subject took Patti by surprise.

"A little. I think," Patti answered quietly.

"I'm sure he'll find someone. I know you'll help

him. I think Joe would like it better if he had someone, a special girl."

"I think you're right."

"Patti, I'm sorry about the way I acted when you got pregnant," Joan said, once again jumping to a different subject. "Sometimes a person can be very stupid and can't help it. I never meant to hurt you or do anything to drive us apart. Can you forgive me?"

Patti just stared at her withering mother. She had been thrown by Joan's directness, and she didn't know how to answer her. She needed time to think. But there was no more time.

"I don't want to leave with this on my conscience," Joan said, pressing for a response from Patti.

"It's in the past, Mom." Patti couldn't think of what else to say.

"Your father is a very brave man, Patti. But he's lonely. He . . ." Joan's voice suddenly broke off. Her eyes glazed over. She started to examine her fingernails as if she had never seen them before. She seemed lost.

"Mom?" Patti called to her mother, trying to arouse her. "Mom?" Still no answer. Her voice hit a note of desperation as she cried out, "Mom?"

"Is Joe dating?" Joan asked again, now lucid.

"I think so," said Patti, trying to keep up with her mother's drifting attention span.

"Patti, your father is a very good man, but he's very lonely. He doesn't have many friends. I want you and Joe to encourage him to remarry." Joan frowned in concern. "He'll die if he doesn't. He needs a woman. Will you do that?"

"Yes," Patti answered. What else could she say? She could never really imagine her father with another woman, and until now, she had never even thought about the reality of such an event.

"He won't listen to me about this, but he'll listen to you and Joe. I have two women in mind." Joan now sounded very determined. "One lives here, the other lives in Florida. Sue Lanchill and Wilimina Garley."

Patti looked down. She didn't like either name.

"Both their husbands are dead," Joan continued. "They were old friends of ours. Willie is my first choice." Joan had obviously spent some time thinking about all of this. "Willie lives in Ocala in her own house. She's about my age. She's very kind, but shy. She's been alone seven years. Maybe if Ben took a vacation, he could pay her a visit, sort of a social call. They could be very happy together."

"I'll suggest it to him. I promise."

"It's not too much to ask?"

"No," Patti agreed.

"I'm telling you this because you understand.

144

You are stronger than Joe. You were always special."

Patti felt uncomfortable at hearing herself compared to Joe. And it felt strange to have her mother now refer to her as "special." She had never told that to Patti before, and Patti would never have guessed that her mother felt this way about her. Why hadn't she said something sooner?

"I almost died giving birth to you. Caesarean section was much more dangerous then. I thought I would have no more children. In labor, I said, 'He better be worth it,' and you were."

Patti shifted her weight, steeling herself. She knew it was time for her to say something now, something she had put off and believed she would never talk to her mother about.

"Mother, I know you've always wanted to know who Benji's father was." Patti paused for effect, as if what she were to say might drive a dagger through her mother's heart. But she knew she had to say it. Joan listened without expression.

"It was Reverend Ansley." Patti spat the words out, her voice cutting and stern. Just the mention of his name made Patti's blood rise. Now, having started, Patti couldn't stop. She couldn't let go. She was like a hurricane now, and nothing could stop her, not even her mother's own frozen gaze.

"Your friend, Ma. The same man that's waiting outside in the corridor now. Maybe we should call him in for a quick reunion now that you know he's part of our little family."

Joan had made no effort to say anything, and this only increased Patti's frenzy.

"He leads your prayer group. He ran *my* Young People's group. You always thought he was so perfect. You said he was a good influence on me." Patti paused, letting some of her anger and fury subside. "Well, it was him, Ma. Reverend Ansley. *Your* friend! And another thing, nobody else knows. Not even Joe, even though you always thought I had told him. But now you know!"

Whatever effect her revelation was having on her mother, the memory filled Patti with an overwhelming combination of emotions. She felt anger and hate, sadness and even shame as she remembered the first time Reverend Ansley had come into her life, and what had happened between them.

Long before John Ansley had actually moved into their community, Patti had heard his name. Her parents had known John's parents from back home, and when John moved to Cleveland, Benjamin and Joan welcomed him to their house with a big dinner. Patti remembered the way her mother had prepared a special meal and had spent all day cleaning and recleaning the house until everything was perfect for this special man. Patti remembered wondering who could be so important.

She remembered walking down the staircase into the living room and seeing John sitting on the couch talking to her parents. He was wearing a navy-blue suit. Patti thought he was one of the most handsome men she had ever seen, and this had surprised her. She had not expected a Reverend to be so good-looking.

She felt an odd, unnamed sensation when he stood up to meet her, and at first, this feeling frightened her. Aside from the age difference, this man was a friend of her parents. And certainly, Patti thought, he could never have anything but feelings of friendship for her.

As time went on, Patti either forgot those initial sexual feelings for Ansley, or she sublimated them. She had never told anyone, not even her best girlfriend, about the effect this stranger had on her. She had found it easier and easier to just regard him as a friend. Only because he was so striking looking did Patti find it easier to tolerate the fact that he talked about many of the same things her parents did—God, faith, and virtue.

Patti remembered the day John came to the house to take her on a picnic. Her parents had taken Joe out of town for the day to see a doctor—a specialist—about a lingering chest cold. Her parents had thought the picnic was a wonderful idea, and even Patti thought it was better than staying home all day. It might even be fun. When John arrived to pick her up, he was wearing an open white shirt and well-tailored black slacks. For the first time in many months, Patti again felt an attraction to him.

She went in John's car to a local park, where they spread out a blanket and took out the sandwiches Joan had prepared for them. Patti thought it was unusual when John started asking her about her boyfriends. She told him that she didn't have a special boyfriend. John had then started to tell her how special she was, and he had reached forward and taken her in his arms to kiss her— not gently, but with so much feeling and passion that Patti felt warm all over, and she made no effort to stop him. At first. But suddenly she did stop him. She told him how confused she was. This couldn't be right. This couldn't continue.

But, John had asked her, didn't it feel good? Yes, Patti had said, a part of her wishing she had lied and said no. But the part of her that yearned to take the good feeling further overwhelmed her sense of reason. She gave in to John, feeling guilty and rebellious at the same time.

John and Patti slept with each other several more times within the next few months. In a way, Patti relished her secret. And John, in private, always told her how much he loved her. He kept telling her that even after she let him know she was pregnant. John had assured Patti that he would work everything out, but he hadn't been specific.

Did he mean an abortion, or telling Patti's parents the truth?

One day, after they had made love, John asked her if she would get an abortion. Patti was shocked. She angrily asked him if he had forgotten the church's stand on abortion, and all the other things he had talked about in church. He had become frightened, and told her he would have to break off their affair. It wasn't right, after all. It couldn't continue.

And, John had said, he would deny their relationship. He would have to deny it. That was the reality. He would never admit to being the father of her child. Patti felt intense hatred and fear. She hated John and she hated herself for being so naive. She didn't know what she was going to tell Joe, her parents, and her friends. The only thing she knew was that she wanted to have the baby. She would have to start a life of her own, away from the suffocating morality of the house she had grown up in.

Patti's secret became a form of revenge, and although she loved her son, she had never stopped hating his father and all he represented, and her mother became caught up in that hate, too. Patti had told herself again and again that she would never tell her mother or anybody who the father was. Keeping it a secret helped fuel her hatred, and she took all that emotion and packed it into her singing and into rock and roll, her refuge from "good" people of good influence. But here she was, finally, telling her mother. Part of her felt cruel, knowing how this news would shatter her mother. But she suddenly wanted to transfer the anger she had lived with so long to her mother and let her feel it. She couldn't wait to see how her mother would handle all of this.

"Well, Ma, what do you think of that?" Patti said, anxious to see her mother break down in rage.

Joan looked relieved, not hurt. Patti's words seemed to have had the opposite effect.

"Good, I'm glad you told me." Joan smiled. "Now I can forgive him."

Patti couldn't believe what she was hearing. Her mother wasn't even angry!

"Now I can forgive him, Patti." Joan paused. "Have you forgiven him?" she asked.

Patti was speechless and confused. Joan slid her hand toward Patti.

"I never believed the terrible things people said about you, Patti. I always believed in you. You were the special one."

Patti felt tears come into her eyes. She hadn't expected this! Part of her wished her mother would stop.

"You were worth it all, Patti," Joan continued, her eyes becoming moist. "You were the one I loved the most. Didn't you know that?" Joan touched Patti's face with her gaunt hand. Her voice was growing weaker as she spoke. "You're a mother too. It's not always easy. You may have done things as a mother that you regret." Joan looked very sad now, and very loving. "Have I done anything so terrible that I can't be forgiven?"

Patti took her mother's hand and kissed the fingers, one by one. She felt herself shiver. Her mother's words had touched her in a way she had thought herself immune to.

"No," Patti answered, her voice cracking.

"There's one last favor I'd like to ask," Joan said.

"Yes?"

"Just one last thing," said Joan, her voice even weaker now.

Patti leaned her ear to her mother's mouth. "Yes? What is it?"

Joan paused. "I want you to join me in heaven. I want you to say that you will be there. Will you?"

Tears rolled down Patti's cheeks as she looked into her mother's eyes. She sank to her mother's breasts. "Yes," she said, her voice muffled.

"Will you?" Joan asked again.

"Yes," repeated Patti as Joan cradled her head.

"Good. I have to conserve my strength now. I'd like to see your father now."

Patti pulled herself up. She was in a daze. Whatever this talk had been, a genuine outpouring of emotion or a theatrical performance, didn't matter. It had succeeded. Patti walked out of the room, closed the door, and leaned against it, exhausted. Her eyes were red. Joe had been pacing back and forth outside Joan's room. When he saw Patti, he jumped to her side. He was concerned to see Patti looking so spent.

"Patti? Is anything wrong? Is she all right?"

"She wants to see Father now," Patti almost whispered, all spirit removed from her voice. Ben Rasnick walked past Patti and Joe and entered his wife's room.

"For God's sake, Patti. What is it?" Joe pleaded. But Patti just started walking down the hall toward the elevator. Joe had to struggle to keep up.

"Patti, what happened?"

"God, I thought *I* was tough," Patti said. "She tried to break me, Joe." The elevator door opened and Patti stepped in. As the doors closed, Patti, all false bravado, yelled to Joe.

"But she didn't get me!"

"Patti! Wait!" Joe called. But it was too late. The elevator door had closed. He turned back to the waiting room, rerunning the conversation in his mind. No matter what Patti said, he could see a change in her. Maybe it was the way her lip had trembled ever so slightly, or the tearstains on her cheeks. Something deep inside his sister had been

touched, something he'd never see would probably never see again. He moment, then sat back down.

The door had closed.

touched, something he'd neve̶r̶
would probably never see again. He ling̶e̶
moment, then sat back down.

The door had closed.

had gone unworn for years. He was straightening his tie in the mirror. Benji, at his side, was trying to do the same.

"Just a sec, Bongo-Boy," said Joe, kneeling to straighten Benji's tie and jacket.

"Are we going to heaven?" Benji asked.

"Grandma went to heaven. We're going to the funeral home."

"Oh," said Benji, forlornly.

"Don't be so disappointed," Joe said playfully.

"Where's Mom?" Benji asked.

"She'll be there," said Joe, wondering to himself if that was true.

The Bonner Funeral Home was a converted Colonial mansion. In the viewing room set aside for Joan Rasnick, a line of friends and relatives waited to pass the bier and offer condolences to the family. The room was dominated by a garish orange-brown carpet. Joan's body rested in a gun metal–gray casket surrounded by floral wreaths. The hymn "How Great Thou Art" played on unseen speakers. Benjamin, Joe, and Benji stood at the end of the receiving line. Reverend Ansley kept busy greeting new arrivals at the door.

Patti was nowhere to be seen.

Joan's brother, Uncle Wes, a bald man in his late fifties, embraced Ben. He wiped his cheeks.

"I'm sorry I wasn't here," Wes told Ben. "I was making plans to come next week. I didn't know it would happen this fast."

"Nobody did," Ben said, trying to console his brother-in-law.

Wes walked over to Joe as his wife embraced Ben. "My little sister, I loved her so. Yet we saw so little of each other. What a strange country this is."

"I know," said Joe, his eyes searching across the room for a sign of Patti.

Wes smiled and bent toward Benji as his wife asked Benjamin where Patti could be. Ben didn't know how to answer or explain, so he just told Wes's wife that Patti had not been feeling well.

Joe saw Bu and Cindy come into the room and stop at the casket to pay their last respects. Dr. Natterson waited behind them. Bu and Cindy approached Joe, who was relieved to see two friends at a time like this.

"Your mother was a nice woman," Bu told Joe. "I know you had problems, but she was always nice to me." Bu embraced Joe, each uncomfortable with the genuine feelings welling inside.

"I didn't think I'd see you tonight. I thought you were playing at the Euc," Joe told Bu.

"We are," said Bu, checking his watch. "But I gotta feeling we're gonna be a singer short. Have you heard from Patti?"

Joe shook his head.

"Damn. I thought you would have. Shit!" Bu felt awkward just then, but he had to ask Joe. "Come on, why don't you stand in for her?"

Joe looked confused. He didn't know if he could.

"We can't cancel, Joe," Bu urged his friend. "The old crowd's going to be there."

Joe understood Bu. They really couldn't cancel. The club had advertised the band's reunion for the past two weeks, and all the people that had supported the band locally would be showing up tonight. It would be special.

"You go to the Euclid," Joe told Bu. "I'll try to find Patti."

Bu gave Joe a hug. He was relieved. He knew Joe would come through for the Barbusters.

Joe walked over to his father and took him aside. "Dad, I love you. But I have to leave. I'll see you later."

"Fine, son," Benjamin said, knowing he could not question Joe further.

Bu followed Joe out of the room. Cindy stayed behind talking with Benji. Reverend Ansley tried to catch Joe's attention.

"Joe, I'm sorry if I said . . ."

Joe didn't bother to listen. He and Bu were out the door.

16 From past experience, Joe knew just where to go find Patti. More than likely, she'd be at the Rascal house trying to beat the lastest video games—trying to forget and escape from her pain. Joe pushed his way through a crowd of goofy sub-teens. He searched up one row of flashing video games and down another. His eyes flitted from one female face to the next. A cocky, drunk kid pushed him back. Joe responded with a sharp elbow to the kid's chest.

Joe found Patti at an Infraspace machine. Dressed in Hunzz leather, Patti stared at the video screen, not playing, not moving. Despite the few drinks she had downed in quick succession, Patti could not keep from reliving her last coversation with her mother. Her mother, Patti thought. How would she get used to the fact that her mother was no longer going to be there? The most obvious and easiest target of her rebellion was gone. She felt the loss of her anger, but right now she didn't feel relieved. She felt empty.

"What are you doing?" Joe angrily asked Patti, jolting her back into the present. "*You* set up the gig at the Euc. They're waiting for you." Joe sounded accusatory.

"Got any quarters? I went through twenty bucks. I'm flat out of money." Patti's voice was devoid of emotion.

"Are you drunk?" Joe asked.

"No."

"Then get your ass up! I'll drive you over."

"You quit, remember?" Patti smirked. "Now I quit!" She stared back at the video screen.

Joe paused before speaking. He weighed his words carefully. Now he could only be honest. "I used to worship you and your black leather jacket. God knows why. But I'm leaving now. I've got something to do." Joe turned to leave.

"You see Dad?" Patti called after Joe.

"How is he, you mean?" Joe asked, looking back at Patti. "The hard part ain't even started yet."

"Where is he?"

"Figure it out." Joe sneered, and he turned and stalked to the door. He pushed his way out of the Rascal House. He had a band to play with.

*   *   *

A letter-lite sign reading WELCOME BACK, BAR-BUSTERS! was the first thing Joe saw as he got out of his car and walked into the Euclid Tavern. The Euc was packed with old, familiar faces. There were friends and fans crowded into the small club. This was Friday night: everyone was laughing, drinking, and listening to the jukebox.

Joe joined Bu, Billy, and Gene as they set up the equipment on stage. Bu greeted Joe with an extended had and a broad smile. Joe shook hands all around. The Barbusters bantered with bar mates as they continued to prep for the show. If Joe had to fill in for Patti tonight as lead singer, so be it. Joe could only feel the energy and enthusiasm of the crowd. After so much recent anguish and sorrow, this felt good.

At the funeral home, Ben Rasnick stood alone beside Joan's open casket. A funeral home employee stood discreetly at the door. Ben bent over his wife. He looked tearily at her face. He couldn't believe this was the last he would ever see of her. Then he noticed that Joan's watch had stopped. He corrected the time on her watch and then wound the knob. This was a futile gesture, of course, but somehow Ben took some comfort in it.

Outside, in the funeral home foyer, Reverend Ansley waited with Cindy and Benji, Wes, Wes's wife, and a couple of other relatives in the darkened entrance.

Patti entered the foyer. She was wearing her black metal gear. On seeing Benji, she dropped to her knees and gave him a hug. The relatives watched with baffled, censorious stares. Patti released Benji, stood up, and was about to enter the viewing room when Reverend Ansley stopped her. He took her by the elbow and walked to a corner of the room.

"Patti. We have to talk. Now that Joan's gone, I feel—"

"Don't you touch me, you bastard!" Patti said. Her tone was mean and unforgiving. "Now that my mother's gone, there should never be any reason for us to see each other again. Ever!"

Patti pulled away, leaving the others to wonder what the commotion had been about. She walked into the viewing room and went to her father. They squeezed each other tightly. Patti was weeping. It felt good to let go.

"Patti, I . . ." said Benjamin, but he didn't continue. They just kept hugging. Father and daughter had been aching to embrace for years. Joan's death had released their inhibitions.

"There was some confusion, Dad. I just got here."

"It feels so strange, Patti. How can it be?"

Patti was moved by her father. Never before had he seemed so human to her. And not until now had she ever felt close to him.

"You're not alone, Dad. We're here. Me and

164

Joe. We'll be there for you now. There are things we can do together. Places, people to visit." Patti was reaching out to her father. The next words came the hardest. "Can you forgive me, Dad?"

They embraced each other once more. For now, there was nothing else to say.

At the Euclid, Barbuster chants got louder and louder as the crowd grew more and more impatient. The group was now on stage. Joe rolled up his jacket sleeves as he moved up to the mike.

"Hello! You may remember me!" Joe yelled back to the crowd.

A chorus of cheers and applause answered Joe. He incited the audience even more with an repetitive guitar refrain.

"My name's Joe Rasnick! Me and my sister Patti used to play here a lot. We're the Barbusters!"

The applause built to a sustained roar.

"Anybody here from Cleveland? Anybody here want to party? Anybody want to rock and roll?" Joe shouted to the audience. Cheers, now louder than before, mixed with raucous applause and yelled greetings. The room was filled with noisy energy.

Joe lunged into the opening chords of "Just Around the Corner to the Light of Day," a Bruce Springsteen song. The band had opened with this song before, but never had the lyrics seemed so meaningful. Joe had been holding a lot back for a long time. Years of pent-up emotion now broke through his voice. As he sang, he sensed the richer and deeper meaning of the song that the events of the past year had given it.

Seemingly from nowhere, Patti jumped on stage and joined Joe at the mike. They sang side by side, one in a black suit, the other in a black leather jacket. The crowd went over the top at the sight of Patti and Joe together.

Patti and Joe playfully bumped their shoulders and then their butts.

They looked into each other's eyes and saw things they had never seen before. They saw acceptance, love, and hope.

They sang of family ties, debts due and paid, and the power of music. Instinctively, Joe and Patti joined hands and raised their arms up together in a gesture that had great meaning for them now. This was not a rock-and-roll pose.

This was rock and roll.